THE SQUITS
FAMILY
HISTORY

John E Wright

CONTENTS

CONTENTS (cont'd)

Other important members of the Squits' household (past and present)
Pets
- Horace (python)
- Semi and Franki (cats)   r.i.p. 2001
- Guinea pigs   r.i.p. 11.2.2005
- Hamsters   r.i.p. 21.5.2005

Key dates
Our birthdays:

Mum Squit	24.3.1957
Barry	18.2.1957
Dave	16.6.1989
Daniel	4.1.1992
Loos	21.5.1999
Mum	25.2.1919
Daddy	5.9.1912 (dec'd 1990)
Barry's mum	22.6.1933 (dec'd 15.12.2004)
Barry's dad	22.11.1930 (decd 22.11.1992)

Wedding anniversary 30.5.1978

Introduction

Welcome to our book. We have had such an interesting and wonderful life, and after circulating our newsletters to many friends and acquaintances, we had the brilliant idea that maybe we should put together our family history and then everyone would know so much more about us.

We are so blessed to have such wonderfully talented children, and a happy marriage – particularly when we read so often of the troubles in the world with many marriages falling apart and people having multiple relationships, and children bringing so much upset to their parents. We thought that we would try our bit to bring a little happiness into the lives of others by sharing some of our experiences in bringing up our children, and how, as a couple, we have been able to make so much progress with our home life, acquiring a good standard of living on the way. Yes, we've had our ups and downs. In this book, you won't get to hear about Barry's recent escapade. Oops! Silly me! Writing that, you've already got a hint that something happened. It was in our Christmas 2005 Niseletter, but we'll save more about that escapade for maybe another book.

My name is Sylvia. I'm better known as mum or mum Squit. My husband, as you've probably guessed by now, is Barry, and I have three children: David (he prefers to be called Dave), Daniel and Lucy (we call her Loos).

Dave is a great singer and lives in a house not too far from a famous pop star's recording studios. I think he will make it in the pop scene – mother's instinct. At the time of writing this, he is about to turn seventeen, but he is very mature for his age. He lives in Wells with our friend's daughter, who keeps an eye on him. More about Dave later. Daniel is amazingly talented in so many ways and you'll learn more about him in the book. Loos is a bright star, but there is not enough room in this first book about our family to tell you all about how clever and lovely she is, so you'll have to wait for the sequel, when I get round to writing it!

One thing I should 'tidy up' at the oustet. The children have been bullied over the years because of their surname, and various acquaintances have suggested that we adopt a different one because of its association with being unwell. Frankly, if everyone with a provocative surname did that, life would be all the more boring and bland! Where would we be if there were no "De'ath", or

"Fear", or "Careless",or "Crapper"? I know children and adults will snigger, but we can't run our lives based on being worried that others think we have a funny surname, can we?

Barry has done very well in his career to date. When you think he started off as a designer in an engineering company after leaving university, and has subsequently gone on to become a very senior manager with B.A.D. Systems and run their subsidiary, N.A.F. Systems (based in Lucerne, Switzerland), you'll already appreciate that Barry is extremely clever. He has been the top sales manager in B.A.D. Mind you, I think Barry has always been very capable. He is very good at fixing things round the house as well, and he has been successful whenever he has chosen shares. Not sure how they work myself, but Barry seems to do well with them.

We have a very big house in Intrinseca, a lovely village in Dorset. It has five bedrooms and lovely gardens. We also have several properties which we have accumulated in recent years, and some of which are in appropriate locations for universities. Always good to plan ahead, isn't it? Barry has a lovely Lexus car, our pride and joy, but I don't drive very often. These days, I can always get a driver if Barry is not around. A taxi can be very useful, but it is not as comfortable as being looked after by a chauffeur.

We have had some great family holidays and we have been to lots of exotic places. We have travelled a lot with the children, so they have very good experience of encountering diverse cultures. We have also used our lovely country cottage near Tenby, in Wales. It has five bedrooms so there has always been plenty of room for us whenever we have stayed there as a family.

We are known to Harrods! We have treated ourselves to their hampers several times, although we had to have a little break from doing so when the children were very young. But you just have to be patient with some things, don't you?

As for me, well, I like to be involved with the local Conservative club, serving on sub-committees. I like to think I have got a good mind for business and think I should probably take some credit for a recent success we had in acquiring the local Women's Institute (WI). Perhaps I shouldn't dwell on that now, but suffice to say, I think you'll appreciate very quickly that we are a very blessed family when you read of all the good things we have and what we have achieved so far. I hope it doesn't make you jealous because jealousy is a bad thing. Your time will come, but celebrate with us as we recall our experiences.

There are so many things to share with you, but this is

probably enough by way of an introduction to whet your appetite. So, turn the pages with me as you learn more of the Squits' family history.

CHAPTER 1

WHITEOUT! HOW BARRY AND ME MET

Now, there's a long story. When Barry was a lot younger, he was the lead singer in a band called Whiteout. They played cover versions of rock music and some of their own material. They mainly played in village halls and community centres. Only once though because they were very loud, so they were hardly ever allowed back a second time!

One night, Whiteout (they chose their name because the guitarist dyed his hair bright white) had a gig in our village in Northamptonshire and I went with two of my friends to see them. It only cost £1 to get in and soft drinks were provided. Anyway, the band were brilliant, and Barry did this one song where he'd rip his shirt open and fall to his knees really earnestly. I just remember being wowed. I think Barry has always been a passionate man. (No doubt the psychologists will say it's something to do with him being a middle child or something like that. Actually, that's a point. Does that still count if you only have one surviving sibling? Sadly, Barry's older brother, Paul, was killed in a motorbike accident when he was only 19. Barry was 18 at the time, and I remember him being devastated. Anyway, I must try to avoid digressing. I have a terrible habit of doing it.) After the concert, when the band were packing away their instruments and the microphone stands and everything else, my friends and I went up to the band members and got chatting with them. Barry asked me out there and then. (I wasn't a groupie" or anything else like that!)

That was around February 1974 when T-Rex, Yes and Deep Purple were going great guns in the world of rock music, along with the glam rock groups like Wizard, Sweet, Mud and Gary Glitter. Those were the days! Elvis Presley was still alive, punk rock had not yet hit us, and we all loved the Queen and the royal family.

Getting back to Barry (I've been told lots of times I'm a flitter, so you better get used to it now, what with all these little asides. Hopefully, it keeps you on your toes!). Barry's 17th birthday was the following Monday night, so we agreed to go out on a date to the cinema. First, we went and got some chips from the local chip shop and we spent ages talking about music, and about telly and what we found funny, and stuff we really didn't like. We got on really well. We both liked "Some Mothers Do 'Ave 'Em", a comedy programme about a man with the innocence of a child, but otherwise utterly incompetent around the house and in work. Barry was annoyed because England weren't going to be in the World Cup for the first time in forever, but I remember being impressed by his sense of humour and generally laid-back approach. As for the film, I don't remember too much about it because we were otherwise distracted for most of it without going into graphic detail – only kissing and that, nothing like what I suspect a lot of folks get up to these days!

I remember Barry having long mousy-brown hair down to his shoulders, and the makings of some sideburns. He had very soft brown eyes and strong eyebrows. Strange what we remember, isn't it? He was quite tall compared to most of the other lads: probably, not quite six foot, and very lean with it – not muscular or anything like that. These days, he looks very different, but that's what happens as we get older.

Barry is a month older than me, but we weren't at the same school. Barry was doing 'A' levels at a town college and I was doing two 'A' levels at our local comprehensive school, my father having decided that it might be better for my social skills after years of private schooling. Barry confided in me that it was a case of having to do the 'A' levels at college because whilst he was in what used to be called the fifth year (year twelve these days, I believe), he had been in a lot of trouble and had tried to set fire to the science block, or at least that is what the teacher who caught him alleged. Ridiculous really! It turns out he and his friends had got some of those caps you used to be able to buy – I don't know if you still can – for toy guns (probably politically incorrect and a criminal offence to have one now). They have the smallest amount of inflammable stuff inside, which, if you scrape them, they cause a small flame as well as the appropriate smell of sulphur. I don't suppose it helped his cause either that when he was caught, it was a very hot day in May and he also had a magnifying glass with him! But, underneath that mischievous and understandable bit of rebelliousness, Barry is very intelligent as was borne out by his 'A' level results, university degree and subsequent career progress.

After our first date, I went to a number of Whiteout's gigs to support Barry. Some were better than others. The band had been started by Neil, the lead guitarist (Barry confirms Neil was responsible for the band name) but Barry had a bit more bezazz about him and it was he who got them doing gigs. Some nights, Neil's guitaring was brilliant; other times, I remember grimacing and holding my ears in some discomfort, not knowing whether he was getting the sound he wanted or was just having a terrible time hitting the right notes. One time I remember smoke began to come out of Neil's amplifier. Fortunately, it was during the band's last song, so they just about made it to the end. Presumably, Neil got a new amplifier because I don't remember it happening again. Another time, I can picture Barry shouting himself hoarse and not being heard because there was a problem with his microphone – I certainly couldn't hear him sing - and I remember him having a very poorly throat for about a week after.

We still keep in touch with Neil via our Christmas Niseletter, but he does not very often contact us. He's never been confident on the phone when I have spoken with him in the past. He does not write much, simply because he lost part of the index finger on his right hand in a freak accident replacing the strings on his guitar (I'm sure that's what he told us).

Barry and I would try and get together at weekends. Barry did very well to pass his driving test when he was seventeen. I think the first examiner must have been overly fussy because Barry is a very good driver, so maybe he was unlucky not to pass the test on the first attempt. When he passed, he had this wonderful old mini which had an endearing smell of old car and worn upholstery, with a hint of oil and musk. Barry used to take me out in it and we had many a good fun outing in that old car.

Obviously, with study demands, it was a case of getting through set pieces of work and creating time to go out with each other. Despite his superficial rebellious streak, Barry was a bit of a softy, which, as I got to know him, attracted me more and more. I discovered that he loved wildlife and nature, and especially loved being in the countryside. (We are not always what we seem, are we?) There was this wonderful area of woodland with some kind of murky pond – I wouldn't call it a lake – in one of the villages Barry new about, which Barry liked to drive me to, and we would walk there. At Charwelton, I think. It was very peaceful and there were lots of different birds flying about. (I've just seen something on the news about birding.) Barry was one of the early bird spotters, able to rattle off the names of different birds very knowledgeably. You can see what I mean when I tell you he's very clever, can't you? Another place he liked to take me to was Everdon Stubbs, a strange name for an area of woodland near a quiet little village in Northamptonshire. (I recall that I once had the opportunity to take part in the Everdon horse trials, but mum and daddy had a social engagement which we had to attend otherwise I would have done quite well because I was a very capable horse rider when I was a teenager.) The woods are lovely there, and very peaceful; same with Badby woods also, and that is only a few miles up the road. All I remember of Badby woods is lots of muddy tracks. It's strange how some things stay in your mind and others don't, isn't it?

Whereas I come from a background where my parents were wealthy, with Barry it was different. His dad was active in the Working Men's Club and his mum worked part-time in the local Co-op store to ensure that they had plenty for little treats, some spending money and enough to help the children with their various interests. Barry had two brothers, one about 18 months older than him, the other two years younger. They lived in quite a nice council-owned house with a good size garden and just enough space for the three children. Mum and daddy owned what had been the old manse for the village church so you can imagine how big it was. We had a massive garden…but I'm jumping ahead now.

So now you know how Barry and I met. Let me tell you about my childhood and my parents in the next chapter.

CHAPTER 2

MY CHILDHOOD

Did I mention I was an only child in the previous chapter? Maybe I edited it out. Mum and daddy were relatively old when I was born compared to these days of teenage pregnancies and my friends having their children in their early twenties. My mother was 38 and daddy was 44.

Mum was born just after the First World War and met daddy when she was 15 and involved in a local athletics club. She was very good at running the mile. All that exercise early in her life has probably helped her to be the healthy and bright person she continues to be – and she always makes me work hard when we play word games. She is trying to get me to do Sodoku puzzles at the moment. Mum is very strong-minded and does not like many of the modern attitudes, especially the bad language on television and all the violence. She thinks the government should bring back physical punishment for wrongdoers so that at least there is a deterrent for when they do wrong. We often argue about that.

Anyway, let me tell you a bit more about my mum. She looks a little bit like me, or is it the other way round? She is a bit shorter than me, maybe five foot two (I don't go in for these silly metrical measurements), not thin, lovely wavy white hair which she keeps cut quite short, about collar length. Mum has very strong brown eyes and can look very stern, which is misleading because, although she has very strong opinions on different things, she is very caring and often helps out many of the senior citizens in our village. She used to be brilliant with a needle and thread before age made her hands a little less dexterous than they used to be. She has made many a wonderful dress for me in the past but, with the advent of global trading, it has been quite easy for some time now to buy a reasonably well-made dress for a modest price. Sad really, isn't it? All these skills we used to learn and have to do in school and for what purpose? (I gather that folks can go into one of the cheaper shops now and buy a pair of trousers for less than £5. Not only that, ladies can buy dresses there for less than £12. Personally, I don't think I would, but one of the ladies in the local

WI assures me that they are good quality.)

Daddy had been very good at distance running when he was a teenager – probably his long legs and lean physique. Unfortunately, he damaged his knee ligaments and had to stop running, but continued to take a lifelong interest in athletics, always following the progress of our middle distance runners. I remember him going absolutely crazy when Steve Ovett and Sebastian Coe emerged as great runners in the 1970s. Anyway, he used to help organise events and provide a helping hand with administration at the club where mum ran, and – as they say – one thing led to another.

Daddy has always had a tidy mind. He helped manage one of the offices of his father's law firm, Screemers and Stonewallis. They were quite a big firm in those days, having seven offices based around Kent and Middlesex, and were eventually bought by one of the larger London firms in the 1970's. Daddy had completed some kind of legal apprenticeship when he was younger and I think he was a Manager's Clerk, or whatever the phrase is. All I know is he had a very important job. He used to sort out wills for people, and sometimes he would have to go to Court on behalf of local businesses where they were sued (claimed against) for faulty goods or services not properly provided. I always found it a bit confusing when he tried to tell me what his job involved, but, as he would say to me, the main thing is that it paid the bills and we did not want for anything, especially when his father died. I think he received a lot of money from his father's estate because he was the sole surviving male heir, his mother having died earlier. He had a much younger sister whom he "saw right".

Daddy was a tall man and not so much thin as slightly gangly, if that's the right word. He was always clean-shaven and I think he looked older than he was. He had very little hair on top, but it kept its dark colour well into his sixties; he used to comb it from one side to the other. His face had this chiselled look about it and he had very clear, almost piercing, steel blue eyes. He also had very big ears, but fortunately not lots of ear hair sticking out of them – unlike some men these days. He always looked very professional when he went to work with his dark navy suit and briefcase. He very rarely brought work home with him and I think the only thing he ever took to work in his briefcase were the sandwiches that mum made and the newspaper to read at lunch-time.

Daddy got quite involved with the local parish council in our village in Northamptonshire after he retired. He held very strong views about shops not opening on Sunday, which seems so strange when you think about the opening hours of lots of businesses these days. (I think he was right. We never know what is good until after we don't have it, do we? It seems to me that life is lived by so many people at such a fast pace.) His views got him into some strong disagreements with other parish council members. He also worked hard to get the local community centre rebuilt and was a keen promoter of young people's interests. He didn't like Barry's type of music but he was always interested in what Barry was doing.

I suppose because I was an only child, and because my parents had a very good standard of living, it was a natural desire on their part that I should go to kindergarten and boarding school for my education. I think generally I had a good time, but mum and I have often had the discussion whether it made me feel less emotionally attached to them. The message we kept hearing when I was an adolescent was that if we wanted to go into a good job when we finished school, we needed to pass our exams - called 'O' levels and 'CSEs' in those days. If you struggled academically in any subject, the CSE was pitched at a slightly lower level. Having said that, it has often struck me since leaving the education system that this is wrong and not what school is all about. In any event, I got 9 'O' levels by the time I finished boarding school and went to the sixth form in the comprehensive school I mentioned earlier.

I always looked forward to the end of a term because it meant that I got to go home to be with my parents, and summer holidays were brilliant because we had eight weeks away from school. I think we had three weeks off at Easter, so that was also quite good.

I must have been about eleven when daddy decided we should move to Northamptonshire. Mum always was happy to go where daddy went. I think that was a good example to me when my relationship with Barry blossomed and we began to think about marriage and what that might entail. I suspect that daddy had calculated that the substantial inheritance he received from his father was likely to outlast my time in boarding school, and that for the benefit of his health (he was mildly asthmatic), moving to the 'rose of the shires' was probably a good move.

I was in boarding school when the move happened, which was quite fortunate having since experienced the stress of getting everything packed and labelled readied for moving house. Mum and daddy decided to buy what had been the old church manse. It was amazing! It was situated on a massive plot of land with lovely gardens, which included a tennis court, a small orchard and an area which had been set aside for growing vegetables. Well, my father fell in love with the place and with the idea of growing his own vegetables! That was only cemented further when a few years later a new sitcom started on the television about a married couple who gave up their busy careers to start what was euphemistically called "The Good Life".

Not only that, the plot backed onto open fields and a paddock which daddy subsequently bought and he had a stable built to house Robina, my horse. When I say 'my horse' I mean she was like my horse. She belonged to Frank Smith, a local builder, but he was on the parish council and was trying to get daddy involved in it because he had a huge respect for my father. He let me treat Robina like my own on the basis that daddy provided the stable. Maybe he did not want to get up early in the morning to muck out and all the other tasks associated with having the horse, but it worked out well for daddy because he never had to pay the vet bills or the farrier when Robina needed shoeing. I think Mr Smith had originally bought Robina as an investment, thinking she would be a good racing horse, but his disappointment was my delight. And I think he got a lot of pleasure from knowing that Robina was such a blessing for me. So you can guess what I got up to the minute I got back from boarding school. Obviously, I had to do some schoolwork sometimes, but more often than not I would spend time with Robina, riding around the field or just telling her what I'd been up to in school, telling her about my friends and things I'd been doing. Horses are very intelligent, but you probably know that. They are also very stubborn and cheeky, and on more than one occasion, I ended up on the grass where Robina had decided she would challenge who was in charge. But she never hurt me, apart from once when she bit my bottom when I'd bent down to check what I thought was a thorn sticking out of her front leg. It turned out to be a strand of straw, but mum says the bruise I got in the process was a wonderful array of yellows, blues and mauves.

Robina must have been about 4 when we began to stable her, and I would have been about 12. Riding lessons were great fun and they probably cost daddy quite a lot of money, but as I began to develop confidence in riding Robina, it seemed that I was quite good, so we began to enter competitions which we knew would take place when I was home from boarding school. Not only that, daddy was happy to pay the school a bit extra so that I could take frequent riding lessons as part of my extra-curriculum activities which, to be fair to the school, were always encouraged. I certainly wasn't going to play netball or be "butch" like some of the hockey-players in my class.

As I developed a degree of competency in jumping fences, it dawned on me that one day I would probably win a competition and that made me feel great, as you can imagine. If you've ever won a competition, or race, or anything like that, you know it's a strange feeling to start with, followed by sheer elation and jubilation – wonderful! Sure enough, I'd been to a number of venues and done my best without getting any prizes, and then one day (as the best stories seem to begin), we were all geared up to go to a small village somewhere near Towcester. I think the event was hosted on a well-to-do farmer's land with a good standard of fences to jump. The 'jumps' were adjusted depending on the category of the entrant. I was 14, so I was in the under-15s. Some of the other entrants were very powerfully built young ladies, some of them from good farming households. Others looked just a little overweight so I reasoned that their horses might not be so happy to be jumping with all that weight on their back. I think I weighed about eight or eight and a half stone (which, as some of our American acquaintances would say, is about 115 to 120 pounds). It's strange: sometimes, you just know things are going to go your way almost as if it is meant to be. I never won any academic prizes and I never had any luck at school fetes or fund-raising events, but that Saturday in 1971 will always stay in my mind as a fond memory. Robina probably sensed I was relaxed and in a good mood. It was a lovely sunny April day, just a little nip in the air, and I think Robina felt in a good mood too, and perhaps thought it would be fun to jump over the fences with me on her back and go as fast as she could. I never felt nervous as she triumphantly attacked each fence and pounded on to the next. Can you imagine how I felt when everyone had done their round and, not only was I one of the two riders with a clear round, but my time was seventeen seconds faster than the runner-up! I was given a prize of fifty pounds in vouchers that I could use towards riding gear from a country stores outlet. I was so proud. You can see that Robina was very important to me during my adolescent years.

Someone else who was important was Linda, who was in the same year and same form as me at boarding school. She had a lovely sense of humour and fun, and had a soft Scottish lilt to her accent. We sat next to each other for most of the school lessons. She was very good with languages and would often mimic a young French lady or sometimes Peter Sellers' Clouseau character from the Pink Panther films, which would get her into mild trouble with the teacher. Fortunately, our French teacher also had a good sense of humour otherwise it could have been more embarrassing not just for Linda but also for me. She was also in my dormitory, so we would often talk about which teachers we liked and didn't like, and would mimic the ones who would get really cross with misbehaving pupils, or we'd talk about what we would get up to when we got back home. Inevitably, that meant me discussing Robina and my riding. Linda liked drama and she was very involved with local amateur dramatics when she was home from school. I didn't have many friends in school, so Linda was very important to me. I had a horrible shock one day when I bumped into our old French teacher at a school reunion about five years after I had finished at boarding school. She told me that Linda had one day hitch-hiked all the way back from Scotland and had been killed in a car crash before she got home. Shocking. It affected me badly.

Locally, I did not have many friends because obviously I was away from the village most of the time, and that was possibly the reason why daddy decided that after I had taken my 'O' levels, I should go to the nearest comprehensive and study 'A' levels there and maybe make some new friends. I can't say I had a brilliant time in the sixth form. I kept my head down and tried to make friends with a nice girl called Susan, but I think a lot of people made up their mind that I was not worth befriending because I'd gone to private school for a number of years and I was therefore well-spoken whereas many of my school colleagues had more of a harsh accent. The main thing is, though, with the few friends who would occasionally meet up with me, I met Barry and he became my best friend so I was able to get through the sixth form without feeling too bad. And even today, I still think of Barry as my close friend. We do have arguments some time but they are never really horrible like some of the marital tiffs you sometimes see on the television.

Some folks would say I had quite a "sheltered" upbringing. I'm not sure what they mean by that. I know all the bad words but I choose not to say them, but I wouldn't say I'm not passionate. I may not have been brilliant academically, but I can't be that stupid because my children are absolutely wonderful, very bright, and very intelligent, so we must have done something right.

I know what I haven't told you (before I move on to some observations about being an only child): when I left boarding school and joined the comprehensive, a friend introduced me to squash, a racquet sport. It took me a long time to get going, but in the end I discovered I could play to a reasonable standard. I think different sporting hobbies come and go when we are quite young and as I went through my teens and got taller and heavier, I didn't ride Robina quite as much as when I had been involved in competitions. At the same time as I stopped entering into riding competitions, I developed as a squash player and joined the leagues at a squash club not too far from where we lived. I started at the very bottom of the leagues and most people beat me easily to start with, but I have a competitive streak, which I credit to mum and daddy. Sometimes I played Barry, and he used to get quite put out when I hit the ball harder than he did. I suspect he thought he could out-hit and out-run me, but he perhaps had not counted on the athlete's genes I had inherited from mum and daddy. I went in for a few competitions. I didn't usually get very far because my opponents were usually younger players who had probably started playing when they were six (or at least very young) and no doubt had received lots of coaching so that playing against someone like me was a very easy match for them. Anyway, I enjoyed the matches and meeting lots of different people. I think I gained a benefit from mixing with different people, and it's probably stood me in good stead for what I do these days in the Conservative Club and mixing with folks from the WI.

We're all different, aren't we, but we have to try and get along.

CHAPTER 3

AN ONLY CHILD

I often wonder what it would have been like to have had a brother or sister, or to have been one of many children. I had a wonderful childhood, I think. When you see all these books in the shops where the authors recall all the horrible things they went through in their youth, and how they were badly treated by their parents, or parent, or carer, you wonder what was going on under your nose and you never knew! Or, you hear of these terrible cases of abuse in children's homes, or boarding schools, and you think 'That could have been me'. We had strong discipline at the school, yes, but we never thought of it as being abuse. The cane was there, but it was hardly ever used, and certainly never in public. That would have been awfully humiliating for anyone of us.

I don't think I was spoilt. It's hard to say because there is no other sibling to compare myself with. All I remember is that I was loved by mum and daddy and I didn't generally feel insecure as I went through adolescence. Maybe I have been blessed with just the right personality. I remember feeling very alone when I first went to boarding school. It was a bit of a shock to my system, I suppose. Hardly surprising when you think I was only seven years old. Kindergarten and infants school had not been a problem because it was only up the road from where we lived in Erith. Boarding school was another matter. I remember that there were a number of boarders who cried and cried for what seemed forever, but I suspect that by the Wednesday after our arrival, we just got on with life, and had giggles and fun as any children would do when left together.

Does it mean you are spoilt if your parents send you to boarding school?

What choice does the child have in the matter? Isn't that a bit unfair If you label someone like that? No, I don't think I was spoilt. I didn't get everything I wanted. I remember that for years at Christmas time, I used to write out my list for Santa Claus (even when I was fifteen), asking for a leather jacket, but I never got one. I always thought I would look quite cool if I had a leather jacket. I didn't dare ask for a leather skirt. Daddy would have been horrified and thought I had turned into some sort of wayward youth. Some of my friends – or rather ex-school colleagues from boarding school - got cars for their eighteenth birthdays…even though some of them had not even started taking driving lessons. I didn't.

Driving a car didn't have the same grip on us in our days as it seems to have on the current youth. (Dave is already pressing me about learning to drive and he is sixteen at the time of me writing this family history. Even Daniel is making hints that he'd like to have a car to be able to drive around the garden!) I started lessons when I finished my 'A' levels so that I didn't disrupt my studies. How Barry managed to fit in all his lessons and his studying is amazing, but then again, he is very clever and very focussed.

I mentioned that I spent a lot of time with my horse (I really shouldn't say that, should I, because the horse was really Mr Smith's – sorry) when I was back home from school, but being an only child, if you don't mix much with other local children – and I didn't – you find other things to fill up your time. I hear of children who spend hours on the computer, playing games or 'chatting', but I was an avid reader. There is a lot to be said for reading. Mum always says it's a great way of keeping a healthy mind, and you're less likely to get Alzheimer's disease or dementia if you keep your mind stimulated with reading and word games. Before she got into Sodoku, she loved to play Scrabble. (Sorry to digress, but have you ever noticed that irritating funny little 'r' that always seems to appear whenever you see the word 'Scrabble'? Maybe the inventor is really worried that someone else is going to steal the idea and make lots of money by inventing another game called Scrabble. I don't really understand all that.) So, where were we? Oh yes. Avid reader. Enid Blyton! When do you ever hear her name mentioned these days? Did you know she was really clever about birds? My friend showed me a book recently that they had found all about birds and Enid Blyton had edited it. I loved all the Secret Seven and Famous Five books, and Mallory Towers. Nice, innocent stuff, which gets your imagination going, and no-one ever gets badly hurt, but they all have an adventure and fun. I suppose it's like an upgrade on Beattrix Potter and her wonderfully illustrated books. Obviously, as you get older, you start to read other stuff, and daddy used to read all these war books by Sven Hassell and Jack Higgins, but I can't say I ever really got into them. (I did like "The Eagle has landed" though. That was great.) Coming back to Enid Blyton, I hadn't realised she was the author of the "Noddy" books until I bought them for Dave when he was young. They are lovely little stories, too, but there is something strange about the character called Big Ears – a little but unnerving if you ask me. Autobiographies and biographies interested me as well: they can be hit and miss, and I don't really want to read all the salacious details about an actor's sexual exploits, or the life of someone in the world of showbusiness who, as soon as pen is put to paper, cannot but use bad language on every page.

That reminds me. When we first moved to the village in Northamptonshire, we didn't have a public library; we had a mobile library! Wow! As Dave would say, "that's a blast from the past". It was good that the local council provided such a facility. I remember you had to step into what was probably an overgrown Ford Transit or some such van and you were surrounded by books. The van smelt a little bit. Maybe it was a combination of 'old vehicle smell' and the musty smell that you get on books when they have been used and re-used, and perhaps exposed to the air on a frequent basis. I could take out two books at a time for two weeks, so it meant you had to get on with reading them which was no problem for me. Nowadays, I can go to the library and have sixteen items if you include CDs, DVDs, videos and books. Amazing, isn't it? Books can often help your memory because you associate them with various things like locations, holidays, sad times, happy times. Many people read when they are on holiday. I know I do. I often think of maybe those rare occasions where I have taken the time to lie on a sun-lounger and engrossed myself in a good novel. Even now I can picture the surroundings, but not only that, it links on to the next step in your memory, which might be recalling going into the town and experiencing the culture of the foreign country you were staying in, or the meal you enjoyed, or the friendly conversation you experienced whilst having a drink in a foreign bar.

I can't say I was ever really too interested in dolls. I did have some. Cuddly toys, I liked them. I had this massive cuddly polar bear. I know they are not cuddly in real life, but it was huge and I felt very protected. Strange what we picture in our mind, isn't it? And then you see on the nature programme the bear pounding on the ice and ripping into a seal! Wouldn't it be nice if all the creatures could get along? Daddy used to say it's all because of Adam and Eve and 'the fall'. Interesting.

When I was seven, mum and daddy decided to try their hand at owning a pet. I don't think it was "them" somehow, but they opted to look after a friend's Labrador for two weeks. Fortunately, I was away at school. Maybe the dog was a replacement for me.

Anyway, mum told me all the goings on when I came back at the end of a term. Apparently, the Labrador was not very old and was male. They had experienced a terrible time with it doing its business in the living room on several occasions, and it had chewed up daddy's expensive work shoes the first night it arrived. Worse than that, my bedroom door was usually left open, and after a few days, there was an unpleasant smell wafting through the house. Not only had the dog weed on my bed and on the floor, it had been grinding its teeth on the bed's wooden structure. The disinfectant had to be got out, all the bed clothes cleaned, the carpet was ruined and the bed had to be scrapped. For me, that was great news, so it worked out well. I liked my bed, but I ended up getting this lovely bed with a nice firm mattress. Also, it prompted mum to decorate my bedroom with some new wallpaper and a new carpet, so the naughty dog's misdemeanours turned out for good. Strange how things like that do, isn't it?

I promised mum I wouldn't dwell on this, so I'll mention it only briefly. Although I was an only child, mum and daddy did want me to have a little sister or brother and mum fell pregnant not long after the incident with the dog. Having decided they would be better off without pets – we did not have a cat or a dog during my childhood years, nor a guinea pig…that would have been nice. My own children loved having guinea pigs. They're lovely little creatures, squeaking and running round in circles. (Sorry, digressing again.) Mum was about seventeen weeks' pregnant when she miscarried. It was a very sad time. My father was devastated. I remember when I came back from boarding school for the summer holiday, he looked as though he had aged ten years. Quite a bit of his hair had fallen out. He looked very thin and very worn. Maybe to console himself, and to 'move on', daddy and I did lots of stuff together, which was great. We went canoeing, we went swimming lots of times, we went on the dodgems together when the fair came to the village.

He also loved the old steam trains, so he took me to Peterborough one day so that we could see them.

Mum was very upset, but received excellent care from the hospital, and the neighbours were brilliant. Her sister, who we never saw, actually made a special visit from Truro just to be with her for two weeks and to make sure dad would be okay while mum recuperated. (I can't remember whether I ever saw her. She probably saw me shortly after I was born, but I think she was a businesswoman and ran some sort of bed and breakfast place, or hotel, down in Cornwall). So, you see, I was nearly not an only child, and despite this knock-back, mum and daddy soon perked up again and got back into their usual routines.

CHAPTER 4

UNIVERSITY CHALLENGE

Mum and daddy having invested so much money in my education, as the time drew near for me to finish studying 'A' levels, the question arose what university I would attend. Mum knows this – because I've since told her – that I was never really bothered about going to university for myself. I think I may be one of those many students who learn in different ways. I've certainly carried on learning since I left the education system, and I am happy that Dave does not wish to go to a university establishment but would rather experience the university of life and express himself through his music. I think Daniel will go to university and probably Loos because they are both so amazingly academically bright. Choices. Where should I go? I hoped to get good grades in the two 'A' levels I studied, namely English and French, but I was not sure of career direction. I always liked English so I thought maybe I could get involved in writing in some way, perhaps journalism, or maybe I could work in a publishing company. At least if I went to university, it would buy me three years.

Barry did very well in his 'A' levels, as it turned out, getting a grade A in "applied maths" and three grade Bs for the other subjects (law, economics and maths). I had hoped that maybe we could go to the same university, then we could spend a lot more time together, although realistically if we had done that we would probably have disturbed each other's studying and got into 'heavy petting' and all sorts of trouble. So I suppose that worked out quite well in a strange kind of way. Barry decided to go to Middlesex and study engineering, and I opted for Southampton. I don't know why but I just did not fancy the idea of going to a big city like London or way up north, and Southampton seemed like a good choice. I always thought Southampton had a nice sound to its name.

I am not sure what I anticipated as regards university life. Maybe I thought it would be like a variation on boarding school, staying in dormitories with lots of other people, getting settled into the discipline of lectures and producing regular pieces of work. I couldn't have been more wrong. I think Barry's personality was more suited to it because he has a bit of a bohemian streak running through him, so the relaxed environment probably worked in his favour.

For me, it dawned on me very quickly that I was unlikely to complete my degree in English. I felt daddy had high hopes of me getting a degree and getting a very well-paid job perhaps in a law firm (he had lots of good contacts in many law firms in the south and home counties) or maybe he thought I would progress and use my language skills and become a notary public, a different kind of lawyer. After the first term, where it felt like I was doing some work but not a great deal, I decided I would try and see out the first year and then break the news to my parents that I would not be completing the degree course.

Southampton is a great city and there are lots of lovely places nearby, as you probably know. The old city walls are down the bottom end of the city, close to the docks, and then there was the floating bridge which went to and from Southampton to Woolston. It wasn't a bridge as such; more of a ferry which cars and pedestrians could go on, operated by some sort of underwater cable which pulled the ferry from one side of the Solent to the other – only about a hundred-odd yards…metres, I suppose, if we have to use metric. It didn't cost much to go on it if you were a foot passenger, and Woolston had lots of nice shops, and it made a day out, or evening out, and was a break from being isolated around the university.

When I decided on Southampton, daddy decided it would be a good opportunity to buy some more property. Also, it meant I would have a degree of independence and he could earn some income if I could find others to share the accommodation with me. As it turned out, initially no other students did share with me. So, following an advert in the local paper, I ended up having a lovely Pakistani lady as a lodger. She came from quite a large family. Her father worked on the docks and her mother ran this wonderful dress shop which was always full of big rolls of linen. I remember going there a few times and having the most wonderful tea. I don't take sugar with my tea, but her mother insisted on providing me with a sweet cup of Ceylon tea and it was gorgeous! Bhavani, that was her name. We didn't keep in contact when I did leave university, but I do recall that she was the perfect lodger: very tidy and clean, and when she made a curry, it tasted amazing. Even better, we managed to get the normal aroma of the house restored much quicker than some Asian homes I've since been in.

The first month I spent in Southampton was, for me, very

lonely. Much as it is nice to live near the sea (that's how I thought of the River Solent) and hear the seagulls squawking, and see the local industries beavering away at the seashore – I think there was an oil refinery nearby, and you could usually make out the cranes from a company called Vosper Thorneycroft (I'm sure Barry could tell you more about their business – something to do with engineering, I think) – it was not the same as the village which I had come to love, having finished with boarding school. I had spent two years getting used to village life: I knew the post office owner, the newsagent, the faces in the local Co-op were all familiar to me, the village chemist was a very friendly man, and I even got to know some of the handymen daddy would call round to fix various things in the house, like the plumber and the odd-job builder and the electrician. So, being somewhat isolated in Southampton in a nice semi-detached with no other students for company, and adjusting to Bhavani's accent, posed quite a challenge for me. Of course I invited students back to our house, but more often than not there were lots of things going on in the university, whether folks were attending student union functions, or gigs, or just cramming into each other's digs for nights of drinking and general revelry. I've never been a particularly big drinker so lots of drinking didn't hold much appeal, and from what had been rumoured, there was a lot of promiscuity going on.   Given my commitment to Barry, I didn't want to get involved in that sort of thing, apart from the fact I was only eighteen at the time. I'd got this hope that maybe Barry and I might get married at some point in the future so I was holding back for him and was not about to blow my innocence on some drink-fuelled meaningless fleshly union.

The thing with writing your own history, it makes you think about some of the things you've been through and what's important to you in your life. Some of the lectures I attended were quite interesting. What perplexed me a little was how some of my fellow-students seemed so desperate to impress the lecturers with their learning that, to me, they appeared rather pompous or pretentious. I don't wish to appear harsh or judgmental, but it seemed a little unnatural. I loved reading, and I was interested in reading around the subject and finding out more about the authors, but I wasn't suddenly going to be a master of English literature, analysing the psychology of what influenced or affected the writings of some of our great writers like Milton, Dickens, Shakespeare or the likes of D H Lawrence, Thomas Hardy or Graham Greene.

I think I slouched through the second term and became more

withdrawn and unhappy. Thankfully, mum picked up on my unhappy moods when I telephoned at weekends to confirm how I was progressing. At the end of the second term I dared to voice what I was planning and was hugely relieved when mum said she thought it was a good idea to finish the third term and the first academic year and then discontinue my university studies. That way, any future employer would appreciate that I had completed one full year of the course rather than abandoning the course without any real perseverance. She was right.

Mum agreed to talk to daddy about it so that there would not be any unpleasant repercussions, and, in any event, the whole exercise had resulted in him acquiring property, a very good investment. Daddy kept the house in Southampton for another ten years, until 1986. Although he did not sell it at the height of the property boom in 1988/9, neither did he get caught out by the subsequent negative equity problem that many folks got caught in during the early to mid 1990's. He had taken a small mortgage to buy the property but the rental income from Bhavani and from subsequent tenants meant that the mortgage was rapidly repaid.

I returned from Southampton mid-June of 1976, an incredibly hot year. Daddy was not a big fan of hot blazing sunshine, whereas I loved hot sunny days, being out in the garden or going out for a bike ride to a local brook and just dipping my toes in the cold water. Daddy was very understanding. We talked about what I would do as regards finding a job, and he promised to talk with some of his legal contacts as well as with different folks in the village who might be able to help.

By this time, daddy was looking forward to retirement. He had decided that as soon as he reached his sixtieth birthday, that was it: he would finish work and enjoy his garden. For years, he had been paying into life assurance policies and they had either matured or were about to mature. Not only that, there was no mortgage on the house and his tax affairs were in order thanks to an excellent accountant friend (who also happened to be on the parish council). So he reasoned that he would enjoy growing vegetables, and he would take a more active part in village life and maybe go out for day trips with mum.

Meanwhile, Barry flourished at university. He was getting good marks for his studies and he enjoyed the socialising. Folks knew he had been in a band so he would occasionally sing with a make-shift group, either in a 'jamming' session or occasionally in a gig. Their motive was that every once in a while it was worth doing a gig for the student union just to get free drinks from the bar and also to get 'favours' when they weren't gigging but were visiting the bar. We kept in touch by letter mainly. Barry had very limited funds to be able to use a public phone, so pen and ink and stamp were our means of communicatuion. During his second year, it got a little easier because Barry shared a house with four other students and they shared the bills, including the phone. Also, by this time, he had worked out that he did not have to work exceptionally hard to get good grades, so he attended fewer lectures and took an evening job with the local newspaper. I'm sure this only served to reinforce his already good communication skills. Although his tasks were mainly general duties, Barry is very observant and picked up lots of useful experience while he was there, I'm sure.   He only needed to spend another year at university. On reflection, perhaps it's just as well that we did university when we did because these days the courses are even longer with many of them having a year out to gain experience in a working environment. So, there I was, nineteen and a half, one year spent at university and needing a job and anticipating that one day soon maybe Barry and I would get engaged.

CHAPTER 5

FAST FORWARD TO MARRIAGE

I mentioned that daddy had lots of contacts in the legal world and that perhaps he held out some hope that maybe I would use my interest in languages to build a career in that environment. At the time, I was not particularly interested in politics but I do remember that Labour were the ruling government of the day and that we had all sorts of problems with strikes and protests. The summer of 1976 was ever so hot. Reservoirs were drying up, folks were saying we were having a drought, but it never looked like the scenes we subsequently saw of Ethiopians with distended bellies and millions dying of starvation as a result of a real drought.

Maybe the combination of the severe heat and Labour being in power conspired against me getting the job daddy expected in a modest-sized law firm in Daventry, a town in ready commuting distance from where we lived and with a good bus service to and from our village. Daddy was disgusted. He had been asked many a time by legal colleagues and professional acquaintances to join the Lodge – freemasons as they call themselves – but he had declined because he thought they were antichristian to the point that their rules and rituals were blasphemous. I always remember him telling me that they believed that god was whoever you wanted Him to be, and they called Him The Great Architect of the Universe, which daddy thought was ridiculous. Daddy thought that in matters of religion, the Holy Bible was what it said, a holy book, and he believed God had revealed Himself as a Creator, and Someone who had chosen a very small nation, the Jews, to be His special people. He also believed that Jesus, the Jew, had come as God's representative and to be the Saviour to Jews and to non-Jews. (I hadn't thought about that for ages, but now that I'm writing this, it's amazing how association brings things back to your memory, isn't it?) Anyway, daddy used to mutter that maybe some of the local freemasons had influenced the partners in the firms he contacted not to support his attempts to get me on board with the firms he knew locally. He didn't bear grudges but I know he was upset, mainly because he thought it was his duty to try and get me employed and using my abilities. My dad was a very honourable man and was always concerned to do the right thing. And his name wasn't Brutus, ha ha!

So, what was I to do? Mum suggested that maybe I could work for a bank, or perhaps I could take forward my interest in journalism. Somehow, being a pushy journalist, hassling for a story for the newspaper, didn't seem to be me so banking had more of an attraction. I had my two 'A' levels, and being of reasonably good intelligence, I thought I stood a chance of getting a good job with one of the big banks. I tried telephoning the local National Westminster Bank branch, which happened to have a branch in our village, but they said that I was too late because they had recruited a number of school leavers as early as April and it was already late June. I don't know why: I was nineteen and a half and I was worried I was never going to get a job. Fortunately, mum had a calm, reasoned approach and suggested that the best thing to do was to go the Careers Service in Northampton.

One Wednesday, dressed in a smart skirt and shirt, and suitably prepared (deodorant, subtle make-up, i.e. no lipstick - you get the picture), I took the bus to Northampton to meet with a careers adviser. The man I saw was very pleasant. I recall that he said he had looked at my qualifications and thought that maybe with my grades – and my completed year in Southampton university – he could perhaps help me apply for a job as a management trainee with Midland Bank. (Later, they were swallowed up by Hong Kong and Shanghai Banking Corporation, otherwise known as HSBC, but many older people will remember the daft advertisements Midland used to run where people would gather round a table and ask 'What sort of a bank account do they want?' Whatever happened to all the funny advertisements? The ones I see now are so serious, or they are just blatantly sexual in content or undertone. Or is that a sign that I am getting older?) The man – I've no idea what his name was – gave me a form to complete. I think it was the bank's standard form, and I had to do the usual: put in my qualifications, what I thought were my strengths and weaknesses, why should I be considered for the job etc. Anyway, you probably don't want to hear about the irksome journey to the bank's regional offices for interview and all that kind of thing. Suffice to say, I was successful in getting an interview, and then I had a lovely interview with this real sweetie whose daughter was in the Salvation Army, and he told me how I reminded him of her, and he thought I would be able to make him proud if he offered me one of the three remaining opportunities to join the bank as a management trainee. He wasn't misbehaving or anything like that…well, at least I didn't think so, and there was never any newspaper stories in years to come that he had preyed on young women…not like you hear on the radio sometimes. No, he was a lovely middle-aged man, and I think he genuinely thought he was offering me a chance. The fact that I did not need to work because daddy was sufficiently well-heeled was not raised in our discussions, but I relished the opportunity for a little independence.

Barry was really proud of me. Daddy was proud of me. Mum was proud of me. I had my first job, so we went out and celebrated in style at the local restaurant, a couple of doors down from the village chemist. I don't remember the meal, but I think it is important to celebrate your successes – even if you can't remember too much detail of how you celebrated!

So it was that late August, after mum, daddy and I had enjoyed an exquisite holiday in very salubrious surroundings in the most gorgeous Georgian hotel overlooking the cliffs near Bideford, I joined the bank. Rummaging around some old papers, I found a box file with my first ever pay-slip in it: £170.15. Wow! When you think about what young people can earn these days straight from school at 16 with their GCSEs, or what they get if they go in for apprenticeships - which seem to be back on the agenda – it's amazing, isn't it?

Being a management trainee meant I had to study the banking exams, which I have to admit were very boring. Barry had done his 'A' levels at the college where the course for the bank exams was to be held, so I presumed it was bound to be good. Instead, the premises turned out to be a late '60's/early '70's-style design and the lecturers were not exactly the most enthusing speakers on their subjects. I had to do four subjects for what were called the conversion course. Maybe it was to be converted to becoming a boring banker with my own bland suit to match a bland personality and to blandly follow the inane mantra that banks got a bad press and were 'hard done by' when they surely were entitled to be paid for providing a banking service to the general public. I didn't do very well when it came to doing the exams, and in the October of the year following my getting the job, I ceased to be a management trainee.

(I'm rushing ahead again. Sorry.)

Meanwhile, Barry was comfortable both with his surroundings and with his progress, and by the time I started my new job, he was beginning his second year on the engineering course. He was quietly confident that not only could he do some gigging and have a good time, but he could also get a first class degree with a bit of hard work just before the third year final exams.

I think maybe there is some kind of formula to understanding the English academic system, and although I don't understand what it is, Barry does in my humble opinion. The more I have read as I have gone on in life, I am inclined to agree that we are all different and we do not all have the same style of learning as we are subjected to – and expected to accept – in school.

Barry is a month older than me. By the time I came to take my Conversion course banking exams, we were both twenty, Barry looking forward to one last year in university and then on with his career, whatever that might be. He was still doing ad-hoc gigs, not with a view to being 'spotted' and being a success in the lurid world of rock 'n' roll, but just to supplement his modest income and contain his costs if he wanted a drink. (He has always liked lager, but I think in recent years he has become quite interested in "real ale". I'm not sure what that means, but with there being so much genetically modified ingredients finding their way into the food chain, it's probably chemically-free, gm-free, organically-grown hops and things that make beer. I'm not claiming to be an expert, but he certainly likes some of these beers with the most odd-sounding names. Whatever happened to Watney's Party Seven and Double Diamond?)

Anyhow, why am I telling you all this? Yes, you may have anticipated it. Barry was anticipating going back to university for his final year and – I don't know whether he was being protective – but one sunny August afternoon, he invited me out for a drive in his Fiesta (the mini had since gone). I thought we were going to Charwelton, but I think I got my bearings wrong because we ended up at this lovely place called Fawsley, not too far from Everdon. Barry parked – or abandoned, might be more accurate – the car and we just walked around this lovely picturesque place. I recall there being some sort of stately home or castle (I'm not totally sure), and there was a pond, lots of sheep grazing, and just the quintessential English countryside to accompany us. I recall there being maybe one other car, but I don't recall bumping into anyone. Anyway, it was just the perfect afternoon for strolling around, girlfriend and boyfriend, with no-one to disturb our conversation or our quietness.

We must have walked for about half an hour, maybe more, when Barry became very awkward, and I sensed in myself that he was about to ask something very serious, and I was hoping it would be the question. For me, it was a very special moment. Barry says he can't remember it, silly thing! He didn't get down on one knee or anything like it. Instead, he went all serious and earnest, and said that he would be very upset if anything came between us, and that he wanted to be sure that when he finished university, he would not be leaving with just a degree. He wanted to be sure that he would be coming home to a wife with his degree. He proposed marriage to me as the evening was coming on and the midges were just starting to do their business of biting my lily-white exposed forearms. The silly thing hadn't bought me an engagement ring or anything like you see in some of the old movies; instead, he gave me what he said was his favourite plectrum as a sign of his commitment to me, and told me that I should look after it until he could afford a proper engagement ring. And, in any event, he would need me to return the plectrum at a later date: he had a gig lined up with the student union for late September! I am not sure whether that qualifies as romantic or not! I think Barry is old school and probably not romantic in the classical sense. He certainly didn't whisk me off my feet and say "Let's elope and go to Gretna Green", or "Come away with me and we'll get married and then let our parents know". But, he's my Barry, and he's the best husband in the world.

Having asked me to marry him, the obvious questions were when and where? Barry has since become relatively well organised but in his late teens/early twenties that description was not well suited to him. We rather liked the idea of going abroad and getting married under licence somewhere exotic like Bermuda or the Bahamas – that was before it became trendy and possibly a little less expensive for young (and older) couples to adopt this route. Mum and daddy really wanted a proper church wedding, and although I did not have any strong beliefs at the time (different now, I hasten to add), I felt it would be more thoughtful to accommodate both of them, especially as daddy was paying for most of it! Barry was quite relaxed about the whole thing. Maybe that was because he did not get too involved in organising the finer detail: his only requirement was to sort out for himself a suit, a decent pair of new shoes and a best man to look after the rings and make sure he got to the church on time.

Being local, the vicar had no problem with us getting married in his church just as long as we attended services in the lead up to the big day and also attended the services for the banns. Daddy knew the vicar quite well, a middle-aged gentleman with wispy grey hair, quite tall and not too dissimilar to daddy in his build and angular looks. He was a keen Coventry City football supporter. I didn't have much idea of what the difference was between a Baptist, Methodist or Church of England, so I was quite happy to get married in the Baptist Church. Nice man, very friendly, and the other people in the church seemed quite welcoming and friendly.

Maybe he had told them. Does that sound cynical? Oh dear me!

Anyway, back to the "when?" Barry had this idea that we should get married sooner rather than later so that I could go and live with him while he finished his university degree. We (daddy and me) did not think that was such a good idea and couldn't work out why Barry was in such a hurry. Barry, the old charmer, said that he did not want to run the risk of someone else getting in quick if he left it any longer because he thought I was extremely attractive and that it was a danger. Mum thought it was a good enough reason and with some trepidation, daddy went along with the scheme. We first discussed it with mum (I don't know where daddy was at the time) mid-September, and after the initial deep intake of breath, mum thought it would probably be better to leave it to closer to the end of May because if it was any earlier we would be so busy getting to know each other that it would interfere with Barry's studies and the outcome of his final exams. (I know it's a long sentence. Doesn't it irritate you when the computer tells you that? I didn't do 'A' level English just for some inanimate machine to dictate how long I should write for! Who determines how long is an acceptable sentence? I'm sure the computer would have a field day if I decided to use Dave's habit of writing in SMS text language! Sorry, digressing again.) We submitted to that idea. It bought us some time to work out where exactly we would live, especially if Barry was sharing a house with other guys from university.

That gave daddy an excellent idea. You remember daddy had bought the house in Southampton when I was at university? By the September when we were discussing the marriage, two tenants were in situ and the income was more than enough to cover the modest mortgage. Daddy thought it would be a very good investment if he were to buy a property near to the university where Barry was studying. In that way, if we decided to move to pastures new were Barry to take a job somewhere else, the property could be rented out to students and the income could service any mortgage. Daddy never said how much he borrowed but the three-bed detached house in Uxbridge cost nearly eight thousand pounds in early 1978 (I think that is right but I can't check it with daddy unfortunately). This is probably the reason why Barry and I have invested in various properties in recent years, but more of that some other time.

I won't bore you with all the intricate details of preparing for marriage. Mum knew someone from the local Women's Institute (WI) who was a genius at flower arranging and she kindly agreed to take up the task of decorating the church with flowers for the big day. We didn't want a choir. No. I couldn't ask Linda to be my bridesmaid because she was untraceable at the time, but was probably somewhere in Scotland doing am-dram. I had no close relatives I could ask so it was all rather pathetic. Thankfully, Sally from work, who I got along with quite well, agreed to help me out. Barry's good friend at the time, Steve, was his best man. Having said that, I think within about eighteen months of being married we lost contact with both Sally and Steve. Sad, isn't it? But that's what happens in life and we just have to move on. Friends are very hard to come by or to keep, it seems.

I had the most gorgeous cream wedding dress with a lovely flowing train and a very pretty tiara and veil for the big day. Barry thankfully did not wear a pin-striped suit: that would have made it look like a business occasion rather than the celebration of marriage. It was a close run thing, though. Fortunately, just as Steve was agreeing on such a suit, one of their ad-hoc band members, Nix (she played bass guitar for them sometimes) spotted them in a department store and knew of Barry's plans. Barry tells me she "gave me a right dressing down" and steered him to a plain but smart dark suit with no stripes.

Daddy looked very regal and dignified in his dark suit on the day and mum looked the typical proud mother letting go of her daughter on the special occasion which was our marriage. She had a lovely, not too ostentatious, hat with an appropriate feather protruding not too far, and wore a nice very light green dress suit. Barry's mother and father looked respectable and his younger brother, Adrian, although he looked a little scruffy, was at least polite and well-behaved.

We had a fantastic day. We said our vows very clearly to each other before all the usual photographs were taken. Daddy took many of them and we ended up with a lovely album from one of the county's leading photographers which daddy had booked. When the ceremony was over, the seven of us, together with the bridesmaid, Steve, and daddy's sister and 'partner', went off to a very posh hotel for dinner and to continue our celebrations.

So, you can appreciate, that from fairly quiet and humble beginnings, the Squits Family began. Barry and I have always been quite happy with each other's company so there has never been a big problem with not having a huge circle of friends. I read once that anthropologists believe we all follow a tribal trait in that we are only likely to have twelve deep relationships in our lifetime so it's very important to be careful who fills the slots. Well, I have Barry, mum, Dave, Daniel and Loos and maybe two or three others at the moment. That allows an opportunity for some other special people I encounter during the rest of my life. Hopefully, I will live a long time, so it's just as well I haven't filled all the slots yet, isn't it? Or is it? Maybe I should give that some more thought.

I must qualify that last paragraph by stating Barry's parents and I have always got on well, and we always enjoyed having them when they were both alive. Sadly, as I write, Barry's mum has since died, and his father having died quite some time ago. We still see Adrian from time to time, but not that often. I always think of him as my brother even though he is Barry's brother.

After our marriage, we had a relatively humble honeymoon by today's standards. Daddy gave us a cheque for a generous sum of money to treat ourselves whilst on honeymoon, but Barry found it very difficult to raise much money for us to go anywhere exotic even though we had entertained (briefly) the notion of getting married somewhere exotic. Instead, we booked into a very quaint hotel not too far from Torquay. We have since toyed with the idea of buying property in the area, but other priorities have conspired against us in that respect. We love the area. It rained the first two days, perhaps because we were still in May, but when you are in love, you don't worry too much about the weather, do you? We spent ten days there and thoroughly enjoyed walking around the area, breathing in the sea air, popping over to Brixham on the ferry and enjoying the fantastic local scenery. We have been there a number of times since but not in recent years. It has probably changed quite a bit. Nowadays, we are more used to journeying further afield when we take holidays, although we do love staying at our cottage near Tenby in Wales.

Those ten days were very special, intimate times, and they helped prepare us for many happy years ahead, as well as for Barry concentrating on passing his 'finals'. I thought I'd leave it to the next chapter to tell you about Barry's career progression, because he has done very well in his career. I am very proud of him.

CHAPTER 6

BARRY'S PROGRESS

Barry, although slightly carefree during his time at university, nonetheless worked hard and certainly revised thoroughly for his final exams. He did enough to get a first class honours degree in engineering but for a very incompetent examiner (either that, or it was malicious). Everything pointed to a first class honours, but as it transpired that was not the final mark he achieved. Needless to say, none of our children will be going there. I am sure most of the professors and tutors, and administrative staff, are very nice people, but Barry is very clever and should have been awarded a higher degree than he received.

Anyway, Barry has told me not to dwell on that point. His first job when leaving university was, I suppose, like lots of first jobs. You have to start somewhere. As a graduate, Barry got offered quite a good salary with an engineering company based near Slough. Although it was not a particularly long journey from the house daddy had bought, we decided that we would like to buy property of our own, not too far away. We eventually settled on a two-bed semi-detached house just on the outskirts of Maidenhead. It meant we were not too far from the Thames, so we could go for lots of little drives at the weekend and occasionally take a picnic. (We have both always been drawn to water.) It also meant we had a degree of independence, which was important to Barry because he did not want to feel that he could not look after me nor to appear dependent on daddy.

I remember Barry had to design an industrial cooker. (I don't understand all that engineering stuff. I've been more interested in the arts rather than the sciences.) I know he worked on the project for several weeks, often bringing home lots of drawings and working late into the night. I presume they must have had a big order to fulfil from some far eastern company, or maybe America. Very hush-hush, you know…important business. Barry made a very good impression with his immediate manager. We invited him round to dinner one evening with his wife. They were a nice enough couple, but not really our sort: he was a bit on the aggressive side and had gone prematurely bald; she was ever so quiet, so it made for a fairly uncomfortable evening. Anyway, the long and short of it is that Barry made steady progress in that company, and eventually became the deputy manager of quite a large department.

Barry toyed with the idea of becoming a freemason, but knowing how much daddy disliked the Lodge, I helped persuade him not to get involved. Barry thought that maybe it might be a good way of networking, particularly as there were already a few of his colleagues who were involved in the local Lodge and were willing to sponsor his admission. Barry thought they were okay because they were active in raising funds for charity and they were a caring fraternity. (From what I've subsequently read, I don't feel comfortable about them at all, and since my own faith has begun to grow, I certainly don't have any time for their multi-purpose, pick-your-own deity.)

Without the help of the "brothers" in the Lodge, Barry made progress on his own merit, and you can imagine my joy when he informed me one evening that he had received a phone call at work from someone who wanted him to come and work for them in their design department. It sounded very exciting: Barry would get to work with the likes of Caterpillar, Rolls Royce, Formula 1 driving companies like McLaren and Ferrari. The new company was based not too far from the Silverstone race-track in Northampton-shire, which was wonderful news because it meant we could see mum and daddy much more frequently than we had been doing since our marriage and move to Maidenhead.

We were not in any hurry at this stage to have children, having married at quite a young age and still working on our careers. That reminds me. You've probably been wondering what happened to my career.) After we married, I tried to get a move to Midland Bank's branch in Maidenhead or the nearest branch, but I'm afraid the bank were not overly helpful because I was relatively young and I think they were disappointed that I had not gained particularly good marks in the bank exams. I resigned. With Barry earning fairly good money, and with a little help from mum and daddy, I did not really have to go to work, which was a blessing for both Barry and me. It meant I could provide Barry with good support and make sure he ate sensibly and did not have pressure in his home life.

We enjoyed living in Whittlebury in a nice four-bed detached house with quite a good sized garden. It was a relatively new house so it meant we did not have to do much maintenance whilst we lived there. We were quite close to Towcester where they had horse racing on a regular basis, and that was fun. Towcester also, at the time, had a lovely market square. Funny sort of place, what with the old Roman road, the A5, going right through it. Strange. That would probably have been around 1984/85.

Barry had a stint at getting involved with Rotary while we lived there - which lasted all of about five meetings. I remember that at one meeting, lots of the folks present got quite drunk and silly and Barry told them plainly that he thought they were all a bunch of ……well, I won't write what he said. Not very nice, and I don't feel it's necessary to use bad language. So…not really his cup of tea. I'm not sure if he's ever really been interested in all the fund-raising and good works they do. Barry is a very private person and gets quite agitated when he sees some of the new advertisements that some charities show on the television. He thinks they are far too harrowing, and he is always concerned about where the money goes. He thinks it's got a little bit gushy, if you know what I mean.

Barry got on very well with the new acquaintances he made in the famous companies. It was during this time that he developed his interest in sales, and his superiors at work spotted that many of the key people in the car and plant companies liked working with Barry, probably because he is very knowledgeable and clever. Although Barry's original brief was to be involved in designing equipment for cars and plant (like these big earth-moving vehicles that you see when motorways or dual carriageways are being built) to help prevent engine fatigue (sounds strange but Barry says it's very important for "performance". I leave it with him - it seems very technical. It soon became clear to the senior management in the company that having been involved in the design process, Barry would be the right man to sell the equipment to the companies. (Oh, that is so frustrating! The computer is interfering again because it thinks I have written a long sentence. I'm sure it makes sense. There must be some way this thing could be set to stop undermining the English language. I can't see Charles Dickens getting very far if he were to write any of his great works in the twenty first century using a computer!)

Barry was a great success. The design stage is very important and there is lots of testing apparently, and fine-tuning, and all that kind of thing. It was very good equipment as well because Barry was very successful selling it to many of the companies involved in Formula 1 racing, and the likes of Caterpillar, and to some of the big car producers in and around Coventry, including Rolls Royce. Very prestigious. The end result was that Barry was made Head of Sales and the company became more and more successful.

They decided to expand and set up an office in Europe. The least said about that the better. Barry was asked for his input only to a limited degree otherwise the office would have done very well, I think. Their excuse was that they wanted Barry to maintain the relationships with their existing excellent clients which he had looked after and those he had won on the back of their recommendations. But it gave Barry a taste for getting about Europe a bit more. The office was based in the north of France, not too far from St Malo. From what I can recall, it was a rather forlorn place which looking like a sprawling town with lots of cranes and activity that you might associate with being near a port. I don't think it helped that the people the company relied on to establish the office did not speak any French and made no bones about what they thought of French people. I mean, how disrespectful can you be?! Especially, in the context of engineering, when you look at some of the wonderful bridges they have built. They are amazing works of architecture.

We were quite settled in Northamptonshire. We had our own routine. Occasionally, Barry and I would go to the local leisure centre and have a game of badminton, or we would pop down to Towcester and have a drink in the hotel (The Bridge, I think it was called. Not sure; it's probably still there and "Under new management" for the hundredth time.) We were also contemplating starting a family of our own so the prospect of moving again, at that time, did not hold a great appeal, and some of the offers were from Scotland and from Northumberland. (I don't know what it is about Scotland: it has wonderful countryside and the lochs, but I always think "cold" when I hear Scotland. I think we'll have to book one of those cheap internal flights and go there for a couple of days and see what it's like.)

Barry was good at his job, so it was not surprising that from time to time he would receive various offers from other companies asking him to join them. A massive multi-national company called B.A.D. systems had come across Barry at a convention he had attended and they contacted him in the spring of 1988, enquiring whether he would be interested in a slight change of direction and working with them on key projects in South America and on the African continent. Barry was interested but explained that he thought it was probably the wrong time because of current projects he was working on, but they left it open to review perhaps at some other time. Little did we know that they were to feature in our lives a few years later.

So, for some time, Barry stayed with the company looking after prestigious clients and meeting lots of famous people. He once met James Hunt, the grand prix racing driver. He thought he was a bit 'loud', but said to me after meeting him that you could see why the women would throw themselves at him because of his long wavy blond hair and his slight drawl despite being so well-spoken. Sadly, he died very young.

For some time, we had tried for a baby, but not making much progress in that area, we opted for the next best thing which I shall now proceed to share with you: a pet…or should I say, pets.

CHAPTER 7

PETS R US

I know it probably seems odd to finish the previous chapter with such a short, dismissive sentence about us trying for a baby and then talking about having pets. But what else could I put? The chapter was about Barry's progress and things he achieved, and tied in with that I briefly hinted how we were getting on in our marriage and where we lived. I am sure you don't want me to bore you with more intimate or intricate details about what we were doing to try and get the desired result? So, as I said, we opted to invest in a pet.

I use the word 'invest' because, like the adverts say in some cars, an animal "is for life, not just for Christmas". Well, probably not for our life, but for their life-span. I always wanted and enjoyed having animals near me. I loved being able to spend time with Robina, not just riding her, but sharing things with her. I wasn't contemplating sharing things with a cat, but I reasoned a cat would be nice company around the house. Bear in mind, I didn't have to go to work because Barry was such a successful manager and was capably providing for me, but then again I didn't spend all day long washing, ironing and running the vacuum cleaner round the house. No. I thought a cat would be good, but I told Barry I would prefer it if we gave a home to a cat who perhaps had not been loved by its original owner rather than sponsoring a breeder. I do love to see pedigrees, but my own conviction is that there are lots of unloved and unwanted animals which could benefit from being in a loving, friendly family environment. There was an animal sanctuary run by some slightly unusual people in Weedon, and so it was that one cold April afternoon in 1988, Barry and I went over to see what was on offer, so to speak.

To be honest, there was not a huge amount of choice. There was a litter of new kittens which all looked slightly scrawny, some old 'moggies' and a few breeds which did not really appeal to me. We came away quite disappointed, but left our details in case anything else turned up, explaining that we were looking for a fluffy kind of cat, probably with some white markings. What we really meant, reflecting on it, is that we wanted a long haired cat with markings around its collar and probably on its paws but we weren't breeders so we didn't know the right language. The couple who ran the sanctuary were understanding, but like I said, they were a bit strange: two women in their mid-forties, wearing the most manly clothing, and one of them having very shortly cropped dark hair which was gradually turning silver. Maybe they were 'partners'. You never know. I can't understand that sort of thing.

Anyway, about three weeks later, Barry had not long got in from work and we were having our evening meal when the phone rang. Two black cats had been delivered to the sanctuary (they weren't from the same family), but they appeared to match our requirement if we wanted to have a look at them. It was late April, so the nights were quite light. It gave us the opportunity to finish dinner, leave the dishes, and drive over to Weedon.

You should have seen them! They weren't kittens, but they looked so nervous and afraid. One of them (Semi – short for Semolina) had a white marking on her left ear and white paws. The other (Franki – short for Francesca) had a beautiful white bib under her chin and her back paws were white. They were lovely. We were told they were probably about eighteen months old and had been looked after by a vet for a few days without being claimed. The sanctuary, it turns out, had arrangements with a number of vets so that rather than the animals being put to sleep, they would take them off the vets' hands and try and find homes for them. I'm not totally sure how the sanctuary owners funded all this kindness, but they probably had a network of friends and acquaintances that gave them cat food. We were advised to have the cats spayed and injected against cat flu, and a suggested donation was proposed by the owners for the provision of the cats. Barry was very generous. So we acquired these two beautiful cats, Semi and Franki.

Mum suggested that we should butter their paws as soon as we got them home from the sanctuary. The reasoning was that they would have to lick off the butter and in the process become familiar with the smell of their surroundings. Whatever, they didn't run away never to return; that was the main thing. Semi and Franki soon settled into the Squits household. Our local vet agreed that they probably were about eighteen months old. They didn't like having their injections but quickly forgave us.

Semi was a little madam. She was the equivalent of the neighbourhood bully. Not only did she make sure that nobody was allowed into our garden, she also made a point of shooing off any cat that came into a garden or nearby path where she was relaxing or prowling. Even the male cats were nervous of her, and there were some big long male cats in our neighbourhood – probably a special breed; looked almost as if they had been stretched - as well as overfed! But, it was lovely to have the cats. They are very relaxing animals, independent, and will let you give affection as long as it is on their terms.

Franki was a different character altogether. She was quite docile. She didn't tend to be too worried if another cat came into the garden. She would stare at the intruder for a long time, perhaps move around lopingly and settle down so that she could observe from a different vantage-point. It was bliss to be able to go out in the garden and potter around, and, as the sunnier days arrived, to sit at the table with a cup of tea and Country Life, just relaxing, watching the cats.

Franki had the bigger appetite of the two. That might explain why she appeared more docile. Semi would wolf down some food, as much as she needed, then she would be off to look after her patch and ensure that no-one stepped out of line by coming onto her territory. Franki liked treats, but you never knew whether Semi would be that bothered if she was offered them, be it cream or a bit of chicken. They both had lovely coats and we are sure they would have won prizes if we had shown them – perhaps put them in a non-pedigree category.

It should have dawned on me earlier that cats are natural predators and that their instinct is to kill rodents. They are preternatural pest-controllers. Sure enough, in the summer we had a procession of dead mice, the odd vole, a little rabbit (that was very distressing), and several blackbirds and the odd sparrow brought into either the living room or displayed victoriously on the patio. Cats have this really disturbing habit of not killing birds instantly and then pawing and flicking them as if it's a game of zig-zag or hopscotch. Eventually, the poor creature dies of a heart attack and is left there motionless while the cat wonders why there is no movement. It's not as if they always eat the bird, although Semi did eat some of the sparrow, I seem to recall. Franki liked to join in with knocking the birds from side to side, but I don't think he had as much success at catching rodents and birds as Semi.

The only inconvenience with owning pets is what you do when you go on holiday. There were a number of catteries within ten miles of us, but we did not know which was best, so when the time came, we turned to the sanctuary for some guidance and a recommendation. The sister of one of the owners ran one of the catteries so you can guess which one she recommended. We were, however, pleased because we thought they must be a family of animal lovers which would mean that Semi and Franki would be well looked after. The time came for us to drive to the airport for our summer holiday late August, but it didn't dawn on us how we were going to get the cats to the cattery. We had thought of putting them both in a cardboard box in the back seat of the car and driving them there, but you will probably think we were very silly or thoughtless to make such a presumption. But we learn from our mistakes, don't we? Needless to say, the day could have been a disaster. Our flight was to leave Heathrow late afternoon for southern Spain and we had planned a leisurely drive down at 10 o'clock. Well, no such luck! The cats would not stay in the box, and then they scratched Barry and he had blood running down his wrist and it spotted the carpet. We didn't know what to do, and then Barry very sensibly phoned a local pet store for some guidance and they told us it would save us a lot of trouble if the cats went in a proper cat basket. So, having attended to that need, we eventually left the house at 10.45 and hastily dropped off the cats at the cattery before doing an about turn and heading off to Heathrow. At least we knew for the next time.

When we returned from holiday, the cats seemed to be okay so there was no problem with putting them in the cattery the next time we went away. We did have a very nice neighbour who subsequently moved into our road – Andrew – and he was a cat lover, so if we needed to be away for a weekend he would keep an eye on Semi and Franki. Nice man. Very high up in the local police force.

Franki had this bizarre habit every once in a while of going absolutely mad, and she would shimmy up the lounge curtains, and hang there like a bat for a few seconds, looking around wide-eyed, before scampering down and whirling around the room. It was very funny, but it didn't do my curtains much good. Fortunately, they were made of very strong material. Very expensive, but durable, otherwise we would have had to replace the curtains at regular intervals.

I had a pet teddy-bear, which I'd had since I was maybe nine. I just had it. I didn't carry it around like a blanket or dummy, but it was there, if you know what I mean. Well, one autumn evening, Semi took it into her head that it was on her territory and she attacked it. I was worried that she was going to tear it limb from limb, but it was so funny. She had grabbed it in a vice-like hug and rolled around the floor with it, kicking it up in the air and then sinking her teeth into its fur. Cats do the strangest things. A fearsome, one-sided battle ensued, where teddy took all her assaults on the chin like the valiant man (or bear) he was without retaliating. A good example of turning the other cheek, I always thought. In the end, I think Semi must have been won over by his patience because after that, she used to snuggle up beside teddy and settle down to rest for the night. I am sure there is a lesson to be learned in that…somewhere.

Semi and Franki both lived into their late teens; I suppose, probably the equivalent of being in their nineties. We still miss them. They became part of the family, and the children grew up with them. They were almost part of the furniture. We looked after them well, and they were fortunate to enjoy generally good health. We did have a scare once with Semi, where we thought she had been poisoned or had perhaps chewed on or partly eaten a poisoned animal. Fortunately, the vets found the right mixture of antibiotics and treatment, so she was okay, but the bill was terribly high!

As the autumn of 1988 wore on, I started to feel more uncomfortable in my clothes, having a bloated, yukky feeling, and my moods began to swing all over the place. Thankfully, having the cats around provided some welcome distraction, but they also began to behave a little strangely around me.

CHAPTER 8

DOES MY TUMMY LOOK BIG IN THIS?

Maybe with the cats taking my mind off getting pregnant, and relaxing much more, it helped me to conceive. Barry and I had wanted a baby for some time but it just hadn't happened. Barry was now more settled in his job; I liked where we lived; I enjoyed having the cats around and pottering about in the garden. So, it came as a bit of a surprise when I started to feel queasy each morning. I thought maybe a bug was going around, particularly as a few of the folks I had walked past in the village had been coughing and blowing their noses loudly and looking generally under the weather.

Then, in the build-up to Christmas, I felt that my clothes were not fitting so well. I was not one for wearing trousers that often, much preferring to go with a nice comfortable skirt most of the time even when I was doing a spot of gardening. One Saturday, I remarked to Barry when we were getting ready to go out and get some Christmas goodies in, whether he thought my tummy looked big. I suppose that was a little unfair because most men would be reluctant to state outright, "Yes, you're looking a bit fat", wouldn't they? Barry probably hedged his bets and asked how I had been feeling. When I said I'd been feeling queasy and having some strange mood swings, we agreed it would be good for me to consult the doctor so I made an appointment for the week before Christmas. Perhaps not the ideal time, but if you're unwell for any length of time, you have to consult the medical profession for their advice, don't you, even if it is just for peace of mind?

Most of the Christmas goodies were in, and Barry and I had sorted out our own and each other's parents' presents, so I toddled off to the doctors on the 19th December for my appointment. After some fairly intimate questions, the doctor, a nice, well-spoken gentleman in his early 50's probably, said to me in a very matter-of-fact way, "Mrs Squit, you are pregnant in my opinion, and I would estimate you are three months pregnant for that matter." I cannot recall too much my reaction. I don't think I was shocked so much as pleasantly surprised, thinking, "Oh, I'd better tell Barry."

Then, as I walked to the shops to buy a few groceries, it began to sink in. By the time I got home, I had gone through a range of emotions from bursting into tears to beaming with joy, to feeling concerned and unprepared, to feeling excited. I was no doubt all over the place when I telephoned Barry to let him know our good news.

Sharing the news of my pregnancy with mum and daddy met with sheer delight. Daddy was absolutely thrilled, mum was overjoyed and her mind suddenly went into overdrive about getting ready for the birth. Daddy was initially concerned whether I was allright. Strange how many men become very worried about their wives' (or partners') or daughters' health when they are told about the pregnancy, as if the lady is somehow in danger. It makes me smile. Maybe it's because they cannot understand how it feels, or grasp the miracle of another life growing inside of their loved one.

I know I probably have some funny ways, but I am not the only woman ever to have had morning sickness and cravings, so I won't bore you with all the sordid details. Suffice to say, I developed a craving for those sweet fruit jellies, "Newberry fruits" I think they were called. I am still rather partial to whatever their equivalent is.

Well, as is the way, pregnant ladies are usually encouraged to attend ante-natal classes, but even before that, you suddenly realise that there is a lot of encouragement and support to be gained just by mingling with other pregnant ladies, some of whom may already have a child or children. I think it did me the power of good because I had never really got too involved in village life up to that point. I knew some folks' faces enough to be pleasant and greet them, but I was not involved in any societies or associations. The local Baptist church had a mums and toddlers group because I saw their advertisement on a notice board on a frequent basis, so I thought that would work out quite nicely when my baby came into the world.

Christmas was very special for us that year as we celebrated the growing life inside me and that we could look forward to a baby in the summer of 1989. (Could make up an alternative cover version of a well-known song with that, couldn't I? "I got my firstborn baby, brought him home from hospital; loved him til we were fit to drop, answered whenever he called…that was the summer of '89 ". Maybe not. I prefer the original.)

We seem to have much milder winters now, don't we, possibly because of global warming or maybe that's a guess by the scientists. I saw a very interesting programme about global dimming, so who knows what's going on with the climate?

Certainly, this last winter has been very cold, so the next thing is we will have folks telling us the ice age is coming! Anyway, my recollection is that Christmas and the winter of 1988/89 was not particularly cold.

My bump got bigger and bigger, and I soon found myself being approached by other pregnant mums who were very friendly and encouraged me to go along to the mums and tots group at the church. I thought that was a bit strange seeing as how I did not have a tot and I was not yet a mum. Some of them had children, but their main reason of getting me there was to have some companionship and refreshments and get to know other mums so I would not feel alone when the time came for my baby to be born. They were lovely people and I think they were the ones who helped me understand the meaning of the word "fellowship". Strange but nice sounding word, isn't it? Has connotations of friendship and caring, and that is what I felt.

I started going regularly to the mums and tots group and thought back to some of daddy's ideas and beliefs, reasoning that maybe I should think about attending church. I discussed it with Barry. He has no strong convictions about faith and the church, although he said he knew one chap in his work who was a very strong Christian whom he had a lot of respect for. I did not delve any deeper, but Barry was happy for me to do what I thought was right, as long as I was happy and found it helpful. You see how kind and good my Barry is? And I would say, that was the beginning of my early steps of faith. Perhaps more of that later.

It would be fair to say that I enjoyed being pregnant. Barry's state of mind or routine didn't seem too affected by it and he was as excited as I was about the prospect of becoming a parent. I think he badly missed his brother, Paul, and to some degree Adrian also. Adrian was, at the time, getting involved with some religious sect, I seem to recall, and that worried not just Barry's parents but also Barry. So, Barry was looking forward as much as me to having responsibility for caring for another family member.

We had a nice spring, and time moved on very rapidly towards the date when my baby was due. I don't recall having a bad back during the pregnancy, and it did not affect my enjoyment of the garden. I kept myself occupied with various tasks. I even started writing a little bit of poetry, just for my own eyes. (I'll have to have a rummage around the garage or the loft one day and see if I can find it. No doubt Dave would have a good laugh at it, or he could even use some of it in his rock group.) We got to June and I remember my bump being very big, all out the front, so I was confident the baby would be a boy.

The anticipated date of arrival was the 14th June. We thought we had everything ready: Barry had painted up the baby's bedroom; we had the cot all in place and a lovely mobile (not to be confused with a phone!); lots of disposable nappies; a couple of baby-grows; some baby milk, just in case. But you're never really ready for the birth of your first baby; you just have to adjust your routine and your planning when it happens.

CHAPTER 9

WELCOME, OUR FIRSTBORN SON

There are some funny sayings that go around, aren't there? Like, "It ain't over til the fat lady sings", or "You can lead a horse to water but you can't make it drink", or "It's just one of those strange things that life throws at you". For me, the arrival of the baby was a case of "Life is one of those things thrown at you by life". I have a slightly different philosophy or approach now, but at the time, even with the best laid plans (as many of us say), we were not ready for the dramatic change which would come our way.

Folks at the Baptist church's mums and tots group were very supportive and great in the days leading up to me going to hospital. Some of them said they would make sure they prayed for me and Barry, and for the safe arrival of the baby, which was comforting. I'm not sure whether I should have expected for the baby to be born with a halo or that I should have entered the maternity ward with an aura of serenity around me. I can say I was not worrying about the detail of how the baby would be born. I had missed the educational film at the antenatal class because of a sore throat, but from what I was told, it was the gory, graphic details of giving birth. Perhaps that was a blessing in disguise, because if I had known the sheer discomfort and pain of trying to squeeze a new life out of a relatively small area from my body (I think you get the drift), my sensitivities and fears would have been extremely heightened.

There must have been at least three other ladies on the ward with me. One lady had been diagnosed with multiple sclerosis about three years previously. It just goes to show that you should not let a medical diagnosis get in the way of living a full and happy life, trying to bring children into the world and enjoying watching them grow up. (I don't know whether she smoked, or had contemplated smoking, marijuana, but I gather it can be very helpful to MS sufferers.) Another young lady – she can only have been about eighteen – seemed very jolly and slightly immature. Her mother and younger sister visited her quite frequently. Very loud. I never saw her husband visit. Regrettably, I presume that she may have been an unfortunate unmarried teenager. So sad, but it was good that her family were supporting her. I don't remember too much about the other lady, but Jo – the lady with MS – was lovely. We got on really well. She lived in Newport Pagnell, and we kept in touch for many years. We even went and had Boxing Day drinks with her one year when our children could only have been about three years old. She already had one daughter who was two and a half, so she was overjoyed that her child was going to get a sibling and not be an only child. Jo had been an only child, and we had a lot of shared experiences so that is probably why we got on so well.

Because I had recently experienced a little loss of blood, I was admitted two days before my due date. I was, therefore, able to build up a little bit of a relationship with Jo who had been admitted a month previously because she suffered from very debilitating tiredness. My baby was due 14th June. That date came and went, leaving me anticipating contractions on the 15th. That date came and went, and what with all the fussing about availability of hospital beds, I think the nursing staff and registrar were beginning to worry about how long I would be in there using up valuable NHS space. I was asked if I wanted to be induced. Feeling relatively relaxed about the whole thing, I declined.

On the morning of the 16th – it was probably only about 6 a.m. – I felt in myself that today was the day. The vacuuming or cleaning of the hospital floors at some ridiculous time in the morning does not exactly allow you to enjoy a lie-in, so I was happily reading the bit in Paradise Lost where Adam is communing with the angel in the garden about what the world was like when God first began His great work of creating the heavens and the earth (I think that's right; it's such a long time since I read that great book) when I suddenly felt this rush and realised the bed was utterly soaked. A quick ring of the buzzer attached to my bed brought a lovely young nurse to me, and the next thing you know I was being taken to the delivery room. I'm not sure what I expected, but it was just like a bedroom with the bed being at a higher setting to what you and I would have it. There was the monitor equipment ready for me to be 'plugged in'. Of course I felt embarrassed at having rather messed up the bed, but I was soon put at ease. (Nurses are brilliant, aren't they? I know we wonder whether they really are human rather than angels. Such a wonderful calling, I think.) What do you do next? It's not as if you can read the paper or finish your book and ask whether everything is finished and all in order, is it? By the time you are ready to give birth, you have had to get used to your private bits being investigated and various nursing staff assessing whether your body is showing signs that you are ready. It does not necessarily prepare you for having your legs put in stirrups so that the midwife can see whether you are "fully dilated"!

After much coming and going, the midwife told me that I was ready. The big, standard issue, clock on the wall said 11 o'clock. I remember that very clearly. I was getting frequent contractions and the midwife told me that, being fully dilated, I should start pushing. "Here we go", I thought.

Very thoughtfully, one of the nurses, who already had our telephone details, phoned Barry at work and suggested that he should be making steps to get to the hospital if he wanted to witness the birth of his first child. Barry was very important to the company so he could not just take time off and leave others to get on with the important tasks that he usually attended to. There was a delay in Barry getting the message from his P.A. because he was in an urgent meeting with extremely important clients – or potential clients – otherwise he would have been with me earlier to support me. As it was, he arrived at 1.15 p.m. to the annoyance, it seemed to me, of the midwife, who was quite cutting in remarking to him that it was nice of him to grace us with his presence, or words to that effect. It was very fortunate because Barry was then able to encourage me through the final steps of the labour. I suspect he had some bad bruising to reward him for the thirty minutes or so I dug my nails into his arms as I valiantly pushed and screamed. Then, at 1.45 p.m., according to the paperwork, David Michael Squit, our firstborn, was brought screaming into the world. I don't think I had many love-bites from Barry during our courtship, but he sank his teeth into my neck and sobbed his heart out, he was so overcome with emotion. David was quickly picked up to be briefly washed and have any gunk cleared from his nose and throat before being handed back to me to hold. He was healthy, a healthy weight as well – over eight pounds – and everything seemed to be in order. We were the proud parents of our very own baby boy.

We had to tell our parents, and of course Barry's mum and dad. Everyone seemed thrilled. Adrian, Barry's brother, was not contactable because he was off in Palestine or somewhere, studying or something with the religious organisation he had affiliated himself to. Mum and daddy came to see us, although daddy's health was not so good at the time. Barry's mum was very pleased to become a grandmother and enjoyed cooing and being with David, but I am not so sure she was really too bothered about children once they got past the age of being totally dependent.

Barry never talked about his mother in any great detail so I don't know if there was some yawning emotional chasm there stemming back to his childhood. As for his dad, I think he was quite chuffed to be a grandpa, but it always seemed to me that he was under the thumb of Mrs Squit senior, as we used to called Barry's mum, otherwise I think he would have seen a lot more of David. It's very sad that David does not remember much of his grandfathers at all.

The folks at the Baptist church were thrilled when they learned of David's safe arrival and encouraged me to take him along as soon as I felt I had got into a routine. There was certainly no pressure, and they explained that the church provided a crèche, so I did not need to feel that if David screamed I would have to leave in embarrassment.

We had a fantastic hamper and wonderful bouquet of flowers from Barry's work, along with some Mothercare vouchers so that we could buy baby-grows and that kind of thing. The church folks gave me a voucher for Adams (a popular children's accessories shop at the time) which was really sweet of them. The local chemist spontaneously gave me a bottle of wine to celebrate with on the first occasion I could get to his shop to buy nappies and the intimate stuff that mothers need after giving birth and beginning breast-feeding. It's amazing what a positive effect the arrival of a new life can have on a community and the out-pouring of kindness it generates. Wonderful!

We brought the cot into our room for the first night, and subsequent nights. Why wouldn't we? We were proud parents. We were also nervous, and wanted to check on David each time he cried. Mum warned us that we would have to get used to sleepless, or at best disturbed, nights, and so it proved to be, but the joy of holding your baby to your chest and sensing the warmth and love and dependency is so powerful…it's affecting me even as I write this. Initially, breast-feeding proved an awkward experience, and like any new mother, after a while you start to fret about whether you can breast feed, and then it all gets overpowering and there are lots of tears and outbursts of frustration. Poor Barry, he bore the brunt of my emotional swings, but he was wonderfully patient. The district nurse visited me regularly, and I visited the local medical centre regularly, for advice and for the usual check-ups and weigh-ins of David. Eventually, we got into the rhythm of feeds, nappy-changes and slightly more sleep each night.

We love each of our three children, but there is always a special place in a mother's and father's heart for the firstborn child.

Maybe you don't agree, but that is what I believe. We were so proud to have David. Barry took a great interest in David and did his fair share of nappy changing and getting up in the night to rock him to sleep or to go through the rhythm of patting or rubbing his back to get rid of wind or colic.

I think it must have taken us about four weeks to get into some rhythm so that we began to recover some of our lost sleep, but you probably have enough details to be going on with and to appreciate what a precious gift we thought our David was.

CHAPTER 10

THE SADDEST DAY OF MY LIFE

When you think about it, my parents were relatively old when their first grandchild was born: daddy was 76 and mum was 70. Daddy must have given up hope of ever being a grand-daddy, whereas I think mum thought that it would all happen when the time was right. I mentioned daddy's health was not very good at the time David was born, and strangely enough, Barry's dad's health was also quite poor.

My parents were quite a bit older than Barry's parents and I always suspected that this was a prime reason why they did not meet up with each other even occasionally. Plus, they each had their own social lives: Barry's dad was quite involved with the Working Men's Club. I think he was treasurer for his local WMC for quite a few years, so it is possible that he drank quite heavily on occasion. His health problem was linked to his prostate, but having had a delicate operation, he seemed to be going on relatively well. He was just coming up to his sixtieth birthday. Barry's mum was slightly younger, but she looked a little older than her years having been a heavy smoker throughout her life – well, certainly since I'd known her.

Daddy kept himself busy locally with his involvement in the Parish Council and he was very well respected by his fellow-councillors. We occasionally popped over to see mum and daddy on a Sunday afternoon so that they could see their grandson and observe his little steps of progress. Daddy was very proud of David, but we noticed in the lead-up to our first Christmas with David that he was looking more and more as if he was worn out. We had no idea that he was seriously ill, so it was a horrible shock when mum phoned us in the middle of January 1990 with the news. Daddy had been to the hospital for some tests and they had found a malignant tumour in his lung. He had never smoked, so we were mystified. Worse news was to come. Just as I was thinking mum was going to tell me that he would need an operation and that we should brace ourselves for the reality that maybe he only had so many years to live, mum shared with me that the tumour was, in fact, inoperable.

Barry was not at home at the time and I really needed some support, but I felt alone and devastated. (If I had thought straight, I could have phoned the good people at the Baptist church and asked them to pray for daddy and mum and me). I was overwhelmed, sobbing my heart out with mum, who had probably had enough time to go through her own personal grief and outburst of tears before phoning me. The conversation was kept brief as mum confirmed that daddy would probably be admitted to the hospital before the end of the month, and realistically he would not be here at the end of February. I sat on the foot of the stairs and buried my face in my hands… and wept… and wept… until I was exhausted by grief. I continued sitting there, mulling over what this would mean. My daddy. He had always been there for me. We didn't see each other every weekend or nearly as much as we should have, and now he was being taken away. I wasn't ready. I didn't want him to go.

Poor little David must have wondered what his mum was up to. I think he must have been at the end of his afternoon sleep and was probably due a feed, but it took ages for me to register the screams of a hungry child unwilling to adjust his routine out of sympathy for another's grief. It may even have helped me to take my mind off the news, or try and re-gather myself and some perspective on my own responsibilities as a mother.

Barry was working late, I suspect on another of the company's important projects. That gave me time to compose myself and phone mum when I had settled down following the shock. I needed to know how daddy was. I was stunned to hear mum say that he was quite relaxed, not too worried, and just a little surprised by the hospital results. Maybe that's what the medical people call 'denial'; I reasoned that maybe it was daddy's way of coping with what I thought was terrible news. I knew he had strong beliefs and convictions, but didn't know that at such a difficult time at this, he was feeling 'helped'. Mum also seemed relatively calm.

We agreed that we would go over and spend time with them on the Saturday, unless Barry really couldn't because of some important work commitment, in which case we would definitely go over on the Sunday. Of course, I was fearful that if daddy was so unwell, how were we to know that he would last til Sunday? Barry did have an important project that really had to be worked on but he saw the seriousness of the situation and how badly it had affected me. He was so kind, and it meant we could spend most of the day with daddy on the Saturday, and maybe seeing little David would take his mind off his circumstances and he could enjoy his only grandchild. It also meant we could talk.

It felt very awkward when we arrived on the Saturday. Barry was very uncomfortable. In some respects, we were completely at a loss what to say to daddy, and just when you want your baby to be perfectly quiet out of respect, all decorum is abandoned and we arrive with a screaming fanfare. Mum was brilliant. (I have to put nice things in about mum because I know she will read this book. Seriously, she was brilliant.) Little David needed a feed, but when that didn't settle him, mum went off into the garden with Barry and David so that I could spend some private time with daddy. It was an unusually mild winter, which is just as well, although not so mild that folks could stay out in the garden for hours with a young child.

Daddy was sitting in his favourite chair with a blanket over his knees and with the Daily Telegraph on the edge of the chair. He had the remote control on the paper and had clicked the television off when he saw me coming into the room. What can you do? I could sense some hot tears running down the edge of my eyes onto my cheeks and catching the corner of my mouth, and my chest starting to heave with sadness. I went over to him and hugged him, and the tears just flowed. He wept also, but more out of sympathy for me, I believe. After a few minutes, I sat in the chair next to him and tried to mumble a "How are you feeling?" I could see through my peripheral vision the patio doors beyond his chair and mum and Barry walking slowly in the garden, engrossed in solemn conversation.

Occasionally, daddy coughed. I had not noticed him do that too often in the past. As I have probably already said, daddy was quite regal and dignified, and not a particularly loud person. His hair was a wispy mixture of grey and white and his brow quite furrowed. His face had that outer beauty of having lived, and been out in the elements in his garden, and having shaved the skin for many decades, it had a slightly leathery appearance. He said that he was very much at peace and looking forward to putting his body to one side. I queried with him what I was supposed to understand by his words. Then, for probably the first and only time I can recall, daddy discussed with me what he said were his deepest beliefs and what had sustained him for years, going right back to when I was born and to when mum had miscarried some years later. I was stunned. I will share only a little detail here. It is true to say that it helped me tremendously to cope with his subsequent death.

Daddy was born just before the Great War of 1914-1918, so he was old enough to be called up to the Second World War in 1939. We never ever talked about his involvement in the War, but he shared a few things with me which astounded me. I have never been much of an historian when it comes to wars, and I admit to knowing very little about the wars. Daddy said he had been a soldier and that he had been on the beaches in Normandy when "everything went wrong", to use his words. He told me he had seen many of his comrades being killed, presumably blown to pieces if "Saving Private Ryan" is a correct account of what happened. Whereas for many people, he admitted, it altered their belief in God and attendance at church, daddy found that on being rescued from such dire circumstances, it strengthened his faith. He felt that in some way he was not worthy of life and it puzzled him why he had been one of the very few who had survived. Most of the men he knew had been issued with a New Testament (from the Bible) when they were 'called up', and after his rescue, he began to read his copy. Most youngsters had gone to 'Sunday School', as they called it, when he was very young, so, like many of his generation, he had some general knowledge of the Bible, including the story of Creation, and great Bible characters like Abraham, Jacob, Moses, Samuel and King David, and some of the parables and sayings of Jesus. Surprisingly, he said, he did not ever remember hearing one Sunday School teacher tell him about God being interested in him or about Jesus being willing to be his friend. (Certainly something I never knew before daddy discussed it with me.)

I said I'd try to keep this brief. Daddy told me that as he read the New Testament, his understanding was that Jesus claimed to be the Son of God and did lots of miracles but was wrongfully convicted and killed by the Jewish leaders of the day. Then, when he read some of the writings of the Apostle Paul, it seemed that Saint Paul was convinced that God punishes sins and sinners but that Jesus offered His life as a sacrifice and as payment for people's sins, like a substitute, for all who would repent and believe in Him, and that if people put their faith in Jesus they could then have a relationship with God Almighty. Probably seems like I'm "preaching to the converted", I know. Anyway, when I asked daddy what he was trying to tell me, he said that he had thought things through and had confessed to God and he agreed he was a sinner and asked Jesus to forgive him and put him right with God because of his sacrifice on the cross. And from that time, he said he knew Jesus as his Friend.

It all seemed strange to me. Daddy said that since that time, he had tried to keep God at the centre of his life, and now that it seemed his time to die had arrived, he was at peace. I only had the smallest amount of knowledge on this subject through my association with mums and tots at the Baptist church. I admitted I did not really understand what he was trying to say. Then he told me plainly. I'll never forget it; he was so confident. I can't tell you word for word, but I can picture him there, in the armchair, saying that he was looking forward to dying and being with "his Lord", and that he knew he was going to be allright because Jesus was his Saviour and therefore he would not have to pay for any of his sins. I ticked him off at that because I didn't think he had sinned; he was a good man, very kind, and hadn't hurt anyone. All he said was "Read the Good Book". (I realised later he meant the Holy Bible.)

You would have probably reacted like me. I felt a bit happier in myself. Not totally convinced about my own emotions, but it seemed daddy was not worried. He was at peace, and that was the main priority. Yet much of my upset that I was about to lose my daddy seemed to be deflected into giving more thought about what he believed.

I remember that mum and Barry came in with David a few minutes later as our conversation was reaching a natural conclusion. I felt slightly perplexed, a bit like we were in the middle of a pause for the commercials to be shown before the programme resumes on the television. I don't know whether I felt cheated of the self-pity that should have taken over so that I could have been morose and unhappy for a lot longer, but I felt as if a rather heavy burden had been lifted. I recall Mum commenting that it was lovely when the sun was out. The next thing you know. we were probably having a cup of tea and a biscuit.

Barry was understandably quiet. It's beginning to coming back to me. In a way, a little upsetting; but, in other respects, comforting. I can't say too much more about the day. I had a young baby, so there would have been the usual interruptions for feeding and the like.

Daddy died just sixteen days later. February 2nd, 1990. He was 77. He deteriorated very badly just a few days after we visited, spending the last few days in the hospital ward receiving excellent care from the colleagues of those who had helped me only months previously when David was born. Mum always used to say that when one life goes, another is born. Maybe David was born in anticipation of daddy going…I don't know. I don't want to be presumptuous about these things.

The next step was to sort out the funeral arrangements. Barry was brilliant. He organised the funeral at the local church, St Thomas's, where daddy was a regular worshipper at their early morning service. Many of the church people honoured his memory by attending, along with quite a few folks from the parish council and some of his former work colleagues. Mum and I had not appreciated that daddy was regarded with such great fondness and esteem by so many people.

The church was quite packed with people for the service which was followed by a modest wake in the parish rooms adjacent to the church. I have to say that mum held up brilliantly on the day. Despite all that daddy told me, I still found it a very sad time. I know he said he was going to be with "his Lord", but I wanted him to be with me. The saddest day of my life? No. I think that was the day I heard from mum that daddy was ill and only had weeks to live. But daddy was no longer in any discomfort. Now, we had to attend to those unpleasant formalities of administering his will so that mum could adjust to a life without daddy.

CHAPTER 11

BARRY, MY STRENGTH

Having organised daddy's funeral, it fell to Barry to liaise with the solicitors whom daddy had appointed as executor. We had presumed that daddy appointed Barry as one of his executors together with a solicitor based in Sittingborne, Kent, so we came in for a slight surprise. It turned out that when we located daddy's will and tracked down (via the Law Society's website) the solicitor who drafted it, he thought that daddy had drawn up a more recent will and had appointed a firm in Daventry. This made sense because Daventry was relatively close to where mum and daddy lived. What with all the properties daddy owned, we thought he must have reasoned that using a local firm would save a lot of hassle if ever his estate needed to be tidied up. That would sum up daddy: very thoughtful of others and well-organised.

Barry was extremely busy with urgent projects, but by great skill in organising his commitments, he was able to help locate all the necessary documentation for the solicitor to help with winding up daddy's estate. In some respects, daddy was very "old school" with all the properties being in his name. He did not want mum to be worried by or exposed to any mortgage lender, so even the wonderful house in the village was in his name. We had to think about what to do with the other properties. Daddy had sold the house in Southampton some years previously but he had kept the house in Uxbridge. He also had two properties in a nice little suburb of Northampton, which I knew nothing about, but then again why should I?

Property prices had dramatically risen because of the then Chancellor of the Exchequer withdrawing what was called 'double tax relief' which entitled each person of an unmarried couple to tax relief on the interest they paid on the first £30,000 of their mortgage. (Strange to think that we do not get any tax relief now.) Lots of couples bought a house urgently because they speculated that they would be badly prejudiced if they did not, which had the effect of hiking up prices in 1988. Just as quickly as prices had rocketed, they suddenly started to slide and I remember the newspapers and television news giving gloomy accounts of the numbers of properties being repossessed by lenders. Horrible experience, I'm sure.

Prices were still falling when daddy died so we were in a bit of a dilemma whether to hold onto the properties or sell them. In the end, out of respect for daddy and so that mum would have peace of mind, we decided on the latter. Barry got involved in some of the negotiation and made sure we got the best price for each of the three houses. He was brilliant. He also ensured that when we encountered a bottle-neck with the National Savings people (daddy had some bonds and savings certificates), that the fuss was soon brought to an end.

Of course, thankfully, little David was oblivious to all the comings and goings of tidying up the estate. In what was a difficult time for mum and me, David helped take our minds off the sadness and helped us to look ahead to the good progress and development happening in his little life. All the tidying up continued as we went into June of 1990. Barry was a great source of comfort to me. Every so often, I would find myself losing control and he would remind me that daddy had not been worried about dying and that he was okay now and I should be happy for him. He tried to encourage me to go along to the church but I didn't feel ready, although I knew in my heart that I would go at some point. Barry has never had much time to become good at D.I.Y. I am sure if he did, he would be very good because he picks up things quickly and is one of these naturally confident and capable people. He is very clever. Nevertheless, as David grew and got used to being in his own room, Barry would try and make time to get away from work a little arlier to be with me through these dark days. Well, they were light actually because it was summertime, but metaphorically speaking, the days were "dark".

Regularly, in between meetings, Barry would telephone me just to check on my progress and to make sure everything was allright, and that little David was going on well. That really helped me. We didn't have to talk about a lot, but I was reassured knowing that Barry was thinking of me. It's the little things that count, isn't it?

We organised a lovely little party for David on his first birthday and made sure mum was able to celebrate with us. It was a little awkward because it was a week day, but there was a bus service to our village but not back, so it meant mum could stay the night with us. (This was not an uncommon occurrence following daddy's death as being in the big house was quite a lonely experience for mum.) Barry got away from work very early and mum and I made a big sponge cake with icing and a big candle and a big number 1 to put on the cake. David was very wide-eyed and excited, but he couldn't eat much of the cake because I was still feeding him and it would have made him very unwell. But he loved the celebrations. We sang 'happy birthday', of course, and made it an occasion to remember.

That day was the beginning of us moving on with our lives, I believe. Tidying up daddy's affairs took a long time. I think if Barry had done the job himself it would not have taken quite as long, but the solicitor's excuse was that "these things have to be done properly". A pity his eventual bill wasn't done properly: there were three typing mistakes and two addition errors, and he had overcharged us even going by the rates agreed at the outset! Barry made sure mum had a reduction in the bill. I'm glad I wasn't within ear-shot when he spoke to the solicitor; I suspect there would have been some strong words. That's the problem with modern business, isn't it? (We had to learn maths and English when I was at school. It was drummed into us that we would never get a proper job unless we passed both subjects. Probably utter rubbish, but at least we know how to add up and check our change when we go to the shops. Folks are so reliant on the till telling them how much change should be given out to the customer that they have forgotten to think for themselves, in my humble opinion.) Attention to detail, when it comes to these sorts of things, is so important.

It was strange settling down to the routine of being a mother but not having one of my parents around. We made a point of inviting mum over regularly, and there was always a bed made up for her to stay the night. I think it is so important that children bond with their grandparents. David thought gran was brilliant. She was always very good with him, probably gave him more attention than I did…but I still had the milk! Ha, ha!

We had great fun in the garden and walking about the village. Mum really liked the village and we toyed with the idea of selling the big house and finding her somewhere nearer to where we lived, maybe in Whittlebury. Barry had been approached by B.A.D. Systems again to see whether he considered that he was ready for another challenge, and one which would involve lots of foreign travel. B.A.D. were very good. They didn't put any pressure on him, but they were convinced of Barry's ability to do a good job for them. That meant there was no sense in moving things around while the job offer was in the air, so we put the idea of mum moving to Whittlebury on hold.

Mum and I enjoyed spending time with David, and occasionally we would get the bus to Badby and have a little wander around that quaint village. Once, we reminisced as I took mum and David up to the woods but we didn't get far with the pushchair, even though it was the height of summer. The ground was all furrowed, so we had to carry the pushchair. David was just beginning to walk, so it was very funny to see him wobbling slowly along the track. The beauty of it was that it gave us time to take in the surroundings and enjoy the peace and quiet, with the birds chirping away, and wind occasionally whispering through the trees. Barry, mum and David had all, in their own way, been a great help to me in coping with the loss of daddy. Barry had been an exceptional source of strength and comfort. He kept on encouraging me to perhaps try and become more involved in the mums and tots group, and mum also thought it was a good idea. I might have been once or twice since David was born, but late August I decided that it would be good for David and for me if I did something about it and went along, and this proved to be the beginning of something very good.

CHAPTER 12

DAVID'S EARLY INTEREST IN SINGING

David, like any other toddler, was into everything as soon as he could walk. We had to buy those funny pretend plug facias to put into the plug sockets so that he didn't keep putting his fingers in – a mother's nightmare! He nearly pulled the corner unit down on himself one time. I don't know what I would have done. We had some lovely cut glass and ornaments of exceptional sentimental value (they were probably worth quite a lot as well, not that I am particularly good at valuing that sort of thing).

Going along to the mums and tots group was a great outlet, and an opportunity to share the load with other mums who were trying to stay calm and in control as their young ones began to grow and take an interest in their surroundings. I was surprised that some of the children attending were not walking even though a few of them were the same age as David. That made me feel quite proud, however, that David wasn't hanging about and was getting on with the job of developing. No stopping my boy, that's for sure.

It was unusual for me going into a church building. We weren't actually in the main area where the services of worship were held, but I was shown in there by one of the mothers almost to make sure I wasn't uncomfortable with being in the environment. They didn't have pews! That was odd, but rather modern, I thought. It looked very comfortable with lots of banners hanging here and there. Very bright and welcoming. Mmm. I probably would go one of these Sundays.

We met in the back room. I think that the church had been modernised in the recent past and spent a lot of money replacing the pews with chairs, carpeting what they called 'the sanctuary', and building an extra building on the back of the original church so that lots of different local organisations could perhaps use it for community purposes. There were toys strewn everywhere, and playmates, and little tables with colouring pencils, papers and bits and pieces for the slightly older children to develop their creative skills. We also had a cassette recorder and some tapes were always to hand with nursery rhymes and little gospel choruses, which made for pleasant background noise. Or so I thought.

I suppose it was in the busyness of preparing for our second Christmas with David that I detected him humming something which I thought sounded familiar. David always took an interest in what was going on. (He is very bright, but in a slightly different way to Daniel and Loos. He is very creative, emotional, reflective and a deep thinker. Probably takes after my daddy, I think.) I couldn't think where I recognised the song from until we went along to mums and tots and realised that he had picked up on one of the gospel songs and was mimicking the tune. Not even eighteen months old! Amazing boy!   That is when I realised that perhaps he had a gift with music, which, as time has gone on, I have felt more convinced that he has. Especially when I consider the various musical activities in which David has been involved during his adolescence.

Barry thought it was great. His son was going to take up the mantle and be a singer, too. He was very happy at that prospect. Secretly, Barry had wanted to be the lead singer in a band like Deep Purple, and tour the world, and enjoy the thrill of singing live to tens of thousands of people. I am sure they made lots of money in their day, but money can easily run out if you're not careful with it. That's what daddy used to say. And, at the end of the day, a singer is a person, and has feelings too, despite becoming famous and earning lots of money and getting lots of publicity.

We wondered whether we would detect the strains of Slade's "Merry Xmas Everybody" before too long, particularly as it was played either on the radio or on the television at regular intervals. (Whatever happened to the man in Slade who wore those terrible high heels with the strange fringe?) Well, it was not to be. Not even part of the melody of "Away in a manger". Barry and I were not, at the time, very familiar with the gospel songs that David and I were hearing on the little cassette player at mums and tots so we couldn't say what the songs were that David was picking up, although subsequently I am fairly sure that one of them was called "Wide, wide as the ocean". Lovely words about the love of God.

And that was the beginning of David's early interest in singing. After the Christmas of 1990, it became more obvious that he was enjoying the music of the songs and, as he learned to speak more words generally, it was such a delight to hear him singing his little heart out as he approached his second birthday. (I must try not to race ahead because after Christmas lots happened.) Mum helped him quite a lot in that respect. She would always talk with him and read stories to him, David the picture of concentration as he sat on her knee. Mum has always liked singing, more of the kitchen-sink variety as she washes the dishes or tidies around the house, not particularly conscious of who is listening. And that was brilliant for David's development and self-confidence. I think if you can happily sing without being self-conscious, it is such a wonderful gift, and probably very good for your health and state of mind. Doctor Sylvia's thought for the day, if you like.

Fortunately, Barry did not get out his old 60's and 70's rock albums and have them blaring away too often or we would probably have been subjected to precocious renditions of "Stairway to heaven", "Allright now", or "Shine on you crazy diamond" and the likes. (You see, I can remember some old songs. songs. I wonder if that gives me extra 'street cred', as Dave would say.)

We made sure that we bought some singalong CDs and tapes to encourage David in his singing, and he loved it when we put them on. We never had any trouble getting him to sleep. If he was particularly unhappy, a little bit of music would soon settle him down. I think it might have been after we moved that Barry picked up his guitar and he would sometimes play it to David if he got home at a reasonable enough time to put him to bed. We bought a nice little rocking-chair around about then and decided David's room would be a good place to site it, so Barry could sit in while David was tucked up in bed, and he could read or play some simple little songs to his boy. The number of times though, in those formative years, I would suddenly be disturbed from my book or television programme and think how quiet it had gone. Barry would be there, fallen asleep in the chair, mouth wide open, proud father with his firstborn nearby. Lovely.

But I've rushed ahead. Things were about to change on the job front, and for the better. That would have implications not only for our immediate family but also for mum.

CHAPTER 13

BARRY GETS A GREAT JOB WITH B.A.D.

B.A.D. Systems had been tracking Barry for a long time, hoping to prize him away from the company whose success Barry had so significantly contributed to. So, it was not too much of a surprise when one cold February evening Barry informed me that he had decided to take up B.A.D.'s offer of employment and that he would negotiate with his firm so that he could start April. The job marked a move away from the design aspect of engineering, although Barry's technical knowledge and expertise would help him in sales.

B.A.D. was a big company with big ambitions to grow their sales in South-America and all those countries which had been part of the United Soviet Socialist Republic (as it used to be called) – you know, the ones which end with "stan". With various countries beginning to shake off the shackles of communism, I presume that the bigwigs at B.A.D. thought that the company was set for very prosperous times. I know that they wanted to get more investment capital and were hoping that, with Barry's know-how and sales experience, recruiting him would be the catalyst to getting a 'full listing' on the Stock Exchange.

It must have been a very important job because Barry was going to get a top-of-the-range Saab as his company car (hopefully before the August), an executive pension, a mobile phone (they looked much bigger in those days, and not everyone had them) and a big rise in his salary. I was going to write something about a declaration but discretion – and a solemn reminder from Barry – has dictated otherwise. The job would entail Barry going all over the world, building up relationships with various contacts and negotiating big deals for the company. Very exciting. Barry confided that he should not tell me too much about the company and his role because a lot of what he did – and still does to some degree – is very delicate. I get the impression a lot of it is to do with mechanical equipment, but it's really special and advanced. He has met all sorts of people since being in B.A.D., but that's another story.

Barry liked Chinese food, but I'm afraid it is not for me. I don't like the thought of all that bright red colouring and lots of sugary sauces. So, we opted to celebrate Barry's success with a meal at an excellent Indian restaurant in Towcester's market square. We had both developed a liking for Indian food and we felt it was important not to let such a success pass us by. I think one of the mums from mums and tots baby-sat for David. Just as well we were not out too long because I remember getting home and having to clear up a load of cat mess. Semi had been having tummy trouble. (It's amazing how we remember things by association, isn't it?)

So, after years of pursuing Barry, B.A.D. Systems had finally got their man. As I indulged in a gorgeous chicken korma, sopping up the sauce with some peshwari naan bread, Barry informed me that because the company's offices were on the outskirts of Reading, it would be better for us as a family to move home. I was not best pleased with that suggestion because I was settled in Whittlebury, I loved going along to the mums and tots, I was comfortable going to church on a Sunday once in a while, and we were close to lots of places I was familiar with from my childhood days. And what about mum? She was on her own. We couldn't just move without taking into account her needs. I felt a degree of responsibility for her, and I still do. Couldn't we just buy another property nearer to where the company was based and Barry could come back at the weekend?

Barry is very clever and has great insight into so many things. I had thought in the past that maybe the more scientific types are not so good with emotional insight and perception, but with Barry that was not the case. With BAD's massive site being on the very outskirts of Reading, it meant we could find a property in a town, or village near a main town that was relatively close to the M4. Barry had done lots of travelling over the years and was confident we would find a nice property which would suit all of us, including mum, in a little village not too far from Hungerford. The name rang a bell with me. Wasn't that the place where someone went crazy with a gun and killed lots of people in the 1980's? Barry acknowledged that it was, but very calmly stated that it was not a frequent occurrence and also we were not going to live in the town itself.

Rather than leave it at that, Barry also pointed out that we could visit the area over the next few weekends and see what we thought of the area. He sounded very optimistic, saying that we would be very close to the M4, Newbury, Marlborough and Oxford, so that if I preferred to go shopping elsewhere I could. Not only that, we would be very close to the River Thames and the Kennet and Avon canal, which gave plenty of opportunities for days out.

Also, if mum planned to stay in Northamptonshire, it would be very easy to get to the A34 from Hungerford, only one motorway junction, and then a fast drive down the dual carriageway to the M40 and onto the A43. He seemed to have it all mapped out in his mind, which helped put my mind at rest a little. I was still a little uneasy about the idea of Hungerford, but we agreed that we should go and see the area and get some property details.

In February and March, we made a number of trips to Hungerford and Marlborough, taking in the Avebury stones and Silbury Hill. I really liked Marlborough's town centre: lovely shops and a quaint church in the middle of the town (I've since been back and the church is now some sort of arts centre and bookshop.) and behind the town centre there were a few quirky side streets and shops. Lots of nooks and crannies to stimulate your curiosity. Hungerford was quite interesting with its long road leading upward to the town centre and several antique shops with extremely expensive furniture for sale. What Barry had in mind, however, was not to live in a town but to help me by finding a nice property in one of the nearby villages where I could perhaps be involved in the community. We looked long and hard at some wonderful cottages about a mile from Hungerford. Villages have some lovely names, don't they? In one little hamlet, there were five pairs of cottages that were quite old but had been modernised, all bearing the most gorgeous thatched roofs. The one we looked at had a strange layout, what with a bedroom on the ground floor and two further bedrooms. It was very quaint and nearby was stunning countryside views. Apparently, together the five pairs of cottages were called the Pepperpots. Lovely. A little bit remote from the nearby village, so I wasn't sure it would be best suited to David, but the nearby villages of Chilton Foliat and Froxfield did appeal.

Having studied the usual eagerly supplied property particulars, we eventually opted for Chilton Foliat, and a lovely four-bedroomed detached property in a quiet cul-de-sac. Even mum was excited. She was weighing up whether she wanted to move to Berkshire, but she confided that she was more at rest knowing that the journey to Hungerford was not a particularly long one even if she chose not to move away from her own village home. Whether we sold our property in Whittlebury or not was thankfully not a great concern because we had the funds to invest in another property and could raise a substantial mortgage loan if we needed it.

CHAPTER 14

CHILTON FOLIAT

What attracted to me this lovely village was that it did not seem to have a huge population and, unlike many greenbelts of Northamptonshire which appeared to have been snapped up and densely (in more ways than one!) developed by building companies, there was a sense of order and space, not too dissimilar to where we had been living peacefully and enjoyably in Whittlebury for several years. There was a good primary school which could accommodate David as he grew older; he would be two years old shortly and I wanted to get him into a nursery and learning to read, write and draw as soon as possible. There was also a very old church, which I've since found out dates back to the fourteenth century and is absolutely laden with history. Very interesting. Hungerford was only about two miles, which meant if worst came to worst, I could always walk there with David in the pushchair, or get a taxi there and back.

We decided we would sell the Whittlebury property and aim to coincide the sale with the purchase of the new property. It didn't quite work out, much to our annoyance, but I won't bore you with the details of our frustration with the estate agents on both sides of the transactions. We were buying from the executors of an estate and, I suppose like a lot of other buyers experience, they were on a different timetable to us. The property had probably been over-priced initially, not taking account of the property market being in a downturn, but with Barry's sensitive negotiating skills we thought we had got an excellent deal. We thought we were realistic in the selling price for our own property until we were on the receiving end of the most stupid and insulting offer by our buyers. Like I mentioned earlier, we were not desperate to sell, but we did not really want to have too much capital tied up indefinitely. The executors wanted a quick completion, which put some pressure on us, and in the end, we chose to complete in the last week of April when we really could have done with leaving it til mid-May or early June. As it happened, that worked out for good, not that we could have anticipated it doing so.

Having only put in our offer in early April, and negotiated an agreed figure shortly thereafter, we then had to work smartly to sort out all the fiddly details associated with a house move. With Barry starting his new job at the beginning of April, working long hours, and staying away most of the week, it was vital that we found a removal company that would sort out all the packing. (It's amazing how much one can accumulate over the years, isn't it?) A very pleasant senior gentleman from one of the removal companies based in Hungerford made the trip to see us and to size up what the move would entail and how many vehicles would be required. I may have been naïve, but I presumed only one was ever needed. In this instance, I was wrong. Mr Jones (what a nice ordinary name that is, isn't it?) suggested that in addition to the usual giant of a removal van, an additional large van would also be required. He anticipated that, unless we urgently began packing – and he had brought with him fifty large self-assembly packing boxes – it would take three of his men probably four days to carefully pack all our worldly possessions in time to move. We opted to move on a Thursday (April 25th, I found it in one of my old diaries), thinking it would make sense to take our time getting things arranged over the entire weekend, and, as regards getting packed, Mr Jones' men were retained by us to ensure that we were ready in time. As an additional service, we were able to retain their services until late in the evening on the day of removal and to help us on the following Friday morning.

It was expensive because it meant that they could not take another job, but we thought it was worth it.

There was no way we would sell our house or exchange contracts in time to complete our purchase so Barry, being the clever man he is, had a friendly word with our bank manager and arranged some further borrowing against the security of our Whittlebury property to supplement our private resources so that we didn't use up all of our capital. It worked like a form of savings in that we would have to make a monthly payment to the bank, but at least we had plenty of money coming in from Barry's job and could leave our other resources untouched.

Leaving behind the Whittlebury property was sad. We had some lovely 'best wishes' cards from some of my acquaintances at the mums and tots group. Even the minister of the Baptist church made time to pop a card through our door which I thought was very kind. I suppose I had visions of moving to Chilton on the Thursday, getting everything sorted out, and then coming back to Whittlebury to tidy up our property. When the last of our possessions was packed into the vans, I took one last look and felt somewhat empty and not a little sad at moving away. That house held lots of lovely memories, and some sad ones. I could see the telephone resting almost forlornly on the round table in the hall, almost as if it could utter the words "You're not leaving me, are you?" Obviously telephones don't speak; they're inanimate objects! But you understand what I mean, don't you?

So, that was it. We hoped the Whittlebury property would sell relatively quickly as we had no intention of renting it out, although that was an option if our buyers could not proceed to completion quickly or pulled out. We had a little upset when they did, but fortunately some other buyers came forward. I think they were young executives; in fact, I think the gentleman was an estate agency manager and his "partner" was a marketing lady, or something like that. They must have taken out a huge mortgage or been very well paid because Barry got an even better offer from them than the original couple who pulled out of buying our house. I just hope they didn't over-stretch themselves; I'd hate to think that they lost the house through repossession. That would have been terrible.

I estimate that Chilton Foliat might have had a population of about 300 when we moved there in 1991. That seems to be born out by a book in the library I glanced through. Lots of interesting details about the village but you have to be careful what you reproduce otherwise copyright laws can affect you, I believe. So, it was a quaint little village. The house had been on the market for some time and the 'For Sale' sign had eventually been removed, so I should not have been surprised by the interest generated when our huge removal van pulled into the cul-de-sac followed by the other van.

The selling agent was there to meet us at 11.30 a.m. and ensured we were able to get in. That could have been very awkward. We did not have any sale proceeds coming in, but with our mortgage loan and the balance already deposited with our solicitors some days previously, there was nothing to delay completion. That meant the purchase price money could be transferred electronically to the executors' solicitors promptly first thing on the Thursday otherwise we would probably have been waiting until 2.30pm or later to get into the property, which we did not want.

We ensured on this occasion that Semi and Franki were in their individual cat baskets and sitting to the side of David who thought it was great fun to be going on a journey with the cats. They may have been teenagers, and very old in cat years, but they certainly put up a fight about going in their baskets. Not for the first time, we were grateful that we had a little first aid kit in the glove compartment, complete with TCP and some plasters. When we were eventually all strapped in, we left some ten minutes after the removal men, overtaking them some thirty-odd minutes later on the M40.

Even with the removal vans, the journey took them a little less than two hours. We arrived well ahead of them, and were able to get the doors opened and plug in a kettle which we had deliberately not packed but had put in the car. The only problem was that we may have been sensible to pack some mugs, but we had no tea, coffee or sugar! The agent, after an initial chat with us and welcoming us to the area, kindly went off with a £10 note from Barry to retrieve some tea, coffee and sugar from a supermarket in Hungerford.

The house had a lovely sized garden at the rear. We did not dare let the cats out. For a start, this was one occasion when I thought the idea of buttering their paws was a good one. The last thing I wanted was to be beside myself with worry about where Semi and Franki had got to. They had been no trouble for years and it would be desperate if they were to suddenly disappear. We were fortunate. The morning had started off cool but it had not been raining. The best option was to leave them in their baskets in the garden whilst we waited for the removal vans and undertook the task of unpacking.

I won't bore you with the details of how grimy the kitchen work surfaces were, or that the property needed a complete overhaul in terms of carpeting and re-painting. I had not noticed, or did not recall, that the house looked so run down. Maybe it was an agent's selling trick to ensure that the house had the 'lived-in' feel to it when we had been on our viewings, but now that it was empty of furniture, the wallpaper looked ancient and hued with nicotine, the light fittings looked as though they may have seen action in the last war what with being eaten through by moths, and the paint on the old-fashioned radiators was flecking and historic trickles of rust could be seen on the pipes leading into the floorboards. Thankfully, the property did not have a cellar otherwise I dread to think what we would have found down there! Probably a pond full of newts and water lilies or sagging ceiling panels and paint full of lead and mercury!

The move was not a relaxing experience, it would be fair to say. It had been a wise choice to get Mr Jones men to help us til late in the evening and the following morning. Understandably, there were boxes which took weeks to unpack, but the stark need to organise what was effectively a complete refurbishment had shocked both Barry and me. Mr Jones seemed to know everybody, from the painter and decorator to the best builders, plumbers and electricians in the area. Even a local carpet-fitter.

We were fortunate in that the double-garage with the property was particularly large and that meant we could store a lot of the boxes in the garage. The only problem with that was that we would still have to unpack at some point, but because the downstairs appeared so bad, we were in half a mind to book into a hotel. It was very upsetting and very stressful. Fortunately, David was no problem. I have to admit that I forgot all about the cats until late that night, poor things.

There was one other thing to be grateful for. The bedroom we thought would suit our purposes had no carpet and no wallpaper! At least that meant we could address that need quickly, probably during the following week or two. Having found some food for Semi and Franki from what we had had the foresight to pack in the car, we sorted ourselves a hot drink, I remember, put David in his bed and took ourselves off to bed for a relatively early night.

The following day, Barry did not have to go to work. We could continue with unpacking, make some phone calls to organise carpet laying, plumbing work and decorating, and we would get to meet some of our neighbours. I was looking forward to that.

CHAPTER 15

MEETING THE LOCALS

Over the next few weeks, we settled into our new surroundings, replacing jaundiced wallpaper, rusty radiators, perished paintwork and rancid carpet. There was lots to do on the house, and lots of people to meet and get to know.

The plumber was quite a character with possibly the most amazing comb-over hairstyle since Arthur Scargill! It seemed to start just above his ears and then there was just a mass of thick grey hair covering an extensive bald patch so that, as he leaned over and beavered away with pipework, this flock of hair would suddenly descend forward. It's a wonder he never set fire to it when he used his blow-torch! In fairness to him, at least he had a warm, jovial personality to go with his unforgettable hair-do. I can't say I remember too much about the other tradesmen except for the carpet fitter who had a bit of a bad mouth on him, which did make an impression, and I had to tell him a number of times to mind his language with such a young child being around. You would think that with a woman being in the environment he would have given more thought to his language, but it seems that bad language has been the order of the day for some years. I don't like it.

We had the living room sorted out very quickly. Having buttered Semi's and Franki' paws, we could let them roam the area and size up the neighbourhood while we concentrated on getting the house in order. Being in the countryside, not surprisingly, we had a steady stream of mice proudly presented to us by Semi. With having a big garden, some of the local birds were in danger of becoming the cats' toys, but that all adds to the mix, doesn't it?

We had some very nice "Welcome to your new home" cards from some of the neighbours in the cul-de-sac, and also one from the church and one from the Womens' Institute (WI), which was a pleasant surprise. I later found out that one of our neighbours was a churchwarden (I think their job is to sort out the candles and welcome people, that sort of thing), so she probably tipped off the vicar. She was also in the WI! It's reassuring that wherever you go there are always thoughtful and kind people, isn't it?

As regards our immediate neighbours, in the adjacent house, if you were to look to the right, lived an elderly couple, probably in their late seventies. I regret I'm struggling to remember the lady's name but the gentleman's name was Arthur. The lady died shortly after we moved in. From what I can recall, the elderly couple went into Hungerford one Saturday morning to do some shopping, and while waiting for the bus, the poor dear had a heart attack and she died there and then! What a quick way to go! Arthur came and told me later that afternoon. Barry was at work and David was having a little sleep, so the best I could do was make a cup of tea and provide some company for him. We thought maybe it was a blessing that his wife had not gone through a long illness or period of suffering, so it softened the blow a little bit. That was the start of a strange relationship. Arthur would often pop round of an evening, and I know Barry found it a little bit waring when he perhaps wanted me to himself. It was the right thing to do though. Poor chap.

On the left, we subsequently became acquainted with a man in his late thirties: another David. We had a shock when we discovered that he had been growing hallucinogenic herbs. It was quite something to witness the arrest of your neighbour. I wouldn't have said David was a menace or threat, but apparently he had made quite a lot of money from trading in his herbs. Never tried them myself. I don't smoke, and Barry generally doesn't smoke, although he does like the occasional cigar…but not when I'm around!

Then, three doors down lived Edna, one of the churchwardens and a very active lady in the local WI, hosting most of their meetings. I grew to like Edna, although some of the WI ladies found her a little overpowering. I think she was a lady who knew her own mind and was not afraid to voice her opinions. Some of those opinions were very strong and controversial, but in fairness to her, Edna was also willing to be put right and consider another's point of view. They don't make them like her any more. She must be nearly eighty now. We still send each other Christmas cards and include our respective newsletters.

Edna must have been a great ally to have on your side but a fearsome adversary. She seemed to have boundless energy without being the sort of character who seems to be going in every direction at once and leaving you drained after you encounter them. She had this wonderful capacity to focus on the task in hand despite having a number of interests. On reflection, I think Edna was at that time someone with great leadership skills, but many of the other ladies missed it. They saw her one or two faults and missed the multitude of her abilities. Edna organised the meetings – or most of them – and seemed to have a cornucopia of connections, which meant that we were never short of interesting speakers. Thanks to Edna, I built up some knowledge of running a social association, which subsequently was to prove very useful.

Perhaps needless to say, but within a few days of moving in, Edna had talked me into attending the Wednesday afternoon WI meeting. When I queried what I would do with David, or what about the various tradesmen coming and going, it was as if the 'problems' were such a non-challenge it was hardly worth discussing. The tradesmen could come and get me if they wanted me, and David could play with some toys in the lounge or wander around her garden. That sort of confidence is inspiring. (Obviously, hindsight then asks what if the tradesmen had stolen any of our possessions, or what if some of the plants in Edna's garden were poisonous, or what if David puts his hands in cat faeces, or has an allergic reaction to something?)

Edna introduced me to the WI ladies, their ages ranging from late thirties to late seventies, so I was among the youngest. They were a mix of well-to-do folks, but very pleasant, friendly and keen to help me get settled into village life. Many of them had been involved in WI since time immemorial, it seemed, so I was treated (!) to various accounts of village scandal, village history, personal exploits of members, etcetera. Not only did I get the chance to learn new skills like turning beer tins into bins, and how to make my own lamp-shades, but the ladies also taught me about the history of the village and the church, and were able to tell me of some of the nice walks on which I could take David. As regards the latter, I am quite a curious person as regards the countryside so I was more than happy to go wandering with David with or without the pushchair.

Being taken under Edna's wing helped Barry concentrate on his new job knowing that someone was keeping an eye on me. Edna was keen to get us along to the church. It seemed rather an imposing building and not as welcoming as the Baptist church we had been to. Barry was not so keen on the idea, but I thought it would be good to take David along. Maybe there would be a Sunday school. There was. Very small: maybe six or seven young children aged between two and ten. We were made welcome. It was traditional but respectful, although not really my cup of tea. But, in fairness to the vicar, he made a real effort – certainly every time we were present – to talk with the children on their level. He was a lovely middle-aged man and his wife was very pleasant too. They had been missionaries in Uganda which sounded very exciting. They had been there when that terrible dictator, Idi Amin, had been ruling the country and indulging in all sorts of corruption for his personal gain at the expense of the health and wealth of the nation. While David was able to do drawing and making things with the Sunday school teachers, I endured the liturgy of Sunday worship. (I wonder if that's where the word 'turgid' comes from?)

When we became better acquainted with the village, we came across the old Methodist chapel which had been closed for many years. I rather fancied myself as a non-conformist believer, but for the time being I made do with going to the "state church". Somehow that doesn't sound quite right.

David and I soon got acquainted with several of the villagers. Glen and Nigel ran a modest garage and workshop for car repairs. They were cheeky but not in a threatening way. They always had time to share a bit of banter with David. Both were married and each had a young daughter, I believe. Both had extra-short hair cuts which made them look a little bit more aggressive than they really were. Isn't it strange how appearances can be so misleading?

We were able to get a newspaper delivered each morning thanks to one enterprising middle-aged lady who took daily delivery of papers at her home at some unearthly hour. I'm not sure how she made any money out of it, especially after paying the young girl who delivered the papers for her. Maybe it was something she thought was a good thing to do for the community. I think Edna informed me that the lady was an author, but I can't say her name stuck in my mind or whether she had made much money from her writings. I bumped into her only very occasionally. Usually, Barry popped along on a Saturday to pay the bill, I think just to establish some kind of connection with village life.

It took a long time for us to make the connection between Bob, the jobbing builder, and the vicar. More of that in a later chapter. Bob was useful at just about anything which required practical application. He did various jobs for us during our time at Chilton Foliat and within weeks of us arriving, we had agreed that he would landscape the garden for us so that the end product would include a wonderful play area for David, a vegetable plot for me, and a purpose-built office towards the end of the garden, complete with electrics so that Barry could work from home if he ever wanted to. We also reasoned that it would make a great selling feature should we need to move in years to come. Bob was always in demand, so it meant that we could get more pressing needs attended to before he would begin the most wonderful makeover of our garden, one of which was to widen and tidy up the side passage to the garden from the front of the house.

Things were taking shape for us. After four weeks, Barry, David and I were settling slowly into village life, many thanks to Edna and a few others. Mum was desperate to come and see the new house and stay with us, but we all agreed it was better for a lot of the property's pressing needs to be attended to first. Our thirteenth wedding anniversary was nearly upon us and I had some news to share with Barry.

CHAPTER 16

HAPPY ANNIVERSARY, DARLING. I'M PREGNANT!

Barry and I did not always go out to celebrate our wedding anniversary, and it didn't look like it would happen having only just moved into the village. Nonetheless, when I let slip to Edna about our pending anniversary, in a very matter of fact way she commanded us to go out for the evening and she would look after David. I'm not sure that I've come across many – if any - ladies remotely like Edna before or since our move to Chilton.

Barry could not afford to have any points on his licence or run the risk of losing it, so we booked a meal at a very nice Indian restaurant in the town and ordered a taxi for the short trip. It meant Barry could drink if he wanted to, although as I've said before, I'm not a big drinker myself; I'm quite happy with an orange juice or a lemonade, and maybe a sweet white wine once in a while.

Having got comfortable at the table, we ordered drinks and some poppadoms while we mused on what dishes to select. Barry was happy with the progress he was making in his new job and had some news to share. In two weeks time, just before David's birthday, he would be going to Nigeria to meet with some business associates with a view to sealing a very big deal. I was disappointed because that meant he would miss David's second birthday, but I understood he could not pick and choose which dates to go if the company had set up the deal for him. There was also the prospect of a nice bonus should he succeed in negotiating the conclusion of the deal. That sounded promising. Other than that, he could not divulge the detail because it was supposed to be very hush-hush.

I responded by saying that I was very happy with our new surroundings. Also, David seemed to have settled in nicely, and I expressed the hope that mum would be able to stay with us very soon. And I had some news. Since early April I had been feeling a little queasy, and during the last couple of weeks I had experienced morning sickness along with the more predictable omission in my monthly cycle. I reached over to Barry's hand, and looked closely at him:"Happy anniversary, darling. I'm pregnant," I said. Barry is such a sweetie. You should have seen the expression he wore, what with having a poppadom half in his mouth, half out; the mango chutney dribbled off the edge and splashed the clean tablecloth. I don't remember Barry's exact response, but it was along the lines of "Wow! That is some news!" Something like that. I sensed he was happy. No doubt, like me, he was thinking what wonderful news that would be for David, who would have a brother or sister to play and grow up with. Barry is, as I have previously indicated, a deep thinker, and was very quiet after that.

We enjoyed our meal in what I felt was a comfortable silence, very relaxed, and pleased to be able to get out and spend time with each other. Knowing that he would be driven home by taxi, Barry celebrated with a number of double brandies. He became very relaxed, I recall, and we talked about all sorts of things during the dessert, reminiscing about his days in Whiteout, our trips to the woods, when David was first born. We really had a lovely evening, and Edna confirmed the good news that David had been absolutely no trouble to look after.

Having indulged in a sherry with Edna to celebrate our wedding anniversary (we did not share our good news at that time), we rounded off the evening by watching some film on the television, or I should say, a small part of the film. I think with all the alcohol he consumed, Barry was in dreamland very quickly. Apart from the fact he had to be in work the following day, he had to get to bed. He is such a reliable worker; always has been.

I anticipated that, by my own calculations, the baby was probably due to be born in January. That was good because the house would be in very good order by then, the garden would be landscaped, mum might have decided whether to move closer to us, and hopefully David would be settled into some routine in a local nursery. I was excited. I was going to be a mother again.

When I telephoned mum the following day, she was excited at the prospect of being a grandmother for the second time. She was also concerned that I should not get too busy or attempt to do too much around the home in case it jeopardised the little life growing inside me. I felt truly blessed and very happy. David was about to have his second birthday, and that would be fun, although I was a little bit concerned when a number of folks kept warning me about the "terrible twos".

We celebrated David's birthday with some of the children from the local Sunday school, David's birthday falling on a Sunday that year. Barry must have been away or working. I recall having some of the Sunday school children coming back to the house after the church service (they had been invited the previous two Sundays) and them all running around in the garden and having a great time. I suspect the cats went into hiding! It would only be a matter of time before David would have a brother or sister to play with and it would be wonderful to see them playing together in such an idyllic environment.

CHAPTER 17

BARRY'S NEW CAR

By the end of that June, we had got through a huge amount of "making good" on the house, to the point where we felt we could call all rooms habitable. Bob, the jobbing builder, had done lots of fiddly jobs for us, including creating a nice, enclosed side access to the rear of the property. That meant we could leave pushchairs and wellies and the like outside of the house without worrying about them getting drenched or blown away. Unfortunately, with having a major wall repair on the vicarage to attend to, and lots of other jobs on-the-go, our planned landscaping was put on hold.

We were enjoying lovely sunny weather. David was in his element: lovely countryside close by; a surrogate grandmother in Edna; gran had been able to come and stay with us a couple of times; a lovely big garden to play in; and we had even bought him a small toy guitar for him to play with. Edna was happy to baby-sit at the drop of a hat, but we were careful not to abuse the facility. It did, however, give us the opportunity to go for out for meals together, and there were lots of lovely restaurants to try in the town, as well as in nearby Marlborough.

I think we had gone to a very nice hotel in Marlborough one Wednesday night to enjoy a meal together. I think it was a Wednesday. I remember there was some football on the television after we came home, and I don't think our football teams played on Thursday nights. That might have all changed now, I suppose, with satellite television. Barry had some news for me. He would be getting his new car on Friday, just in time for the weekend. He was a little disappointed, I remember, because if it had been delayed just a few weeks longer, he would have had a car with the new registration letter. It was going to be a SAAB 9000. How exciting! What colour was it going to be, I asked? Barry didn't know, and I sensed he was not too pleased with the question. It had all sorts of modern features, like air-conditioning, and apparently it was an extremely safe car if Barry or us were ever involved in an accident in it. I must admit, I'd never thought of buying a car with that sort of reasoning in mind.

So, what did the car look like, I quizzed Barry? "Sleek". Mmm. Not sure what that meant. Was that, "sleek" like a nice imitation fur coat (I'm not comfortable about wearing genuine fur), or "sleek" like a well-built leather-upholstered chair...... a proper one, not like these mass-produced leather settees which are always on sale in some furniture stores? I would have to wait til Friday.

Barry often left the house by seven in the morning. We could usually get a cup of tea together before he left, leaving David humming pleasantly in his bed while we snatched a brief conversation. I was looking forward to seeing the new car and what colour it was and whether it looked nice. I think American Independence day had been the week before, so it must have been July 12th (I've checked an old diary for the date). Long, sunny days, so even if Barry worked late it would still be quite light when he got home; light enough to see the car, at any rate.

I am not going to say "It was about 7.30"; all I know is it was not dark, and David was still awake when Barry arrived home with this huge car. I could now understand what he meant by "sleek". It was a strange but pleasant colour: a hint of navy blue and a tinge of black or charcoal. "Midnight blue", Barry has reminded me. I never really thought of sharks as being "sleek", but the car's shape reminded me of a shark. Inside was very plush: cream leather seats, and the steering wheel and dashboard were very different to what we were used to. The steering wheel looked very big, and was a mix of wood and very strong plastic, I believe. The dashboard comprised very nice wood and there seemed to be lots of controls. I would never be able to understand what they all did, but Barry would because he is so clever.

Barry took great pride in showing me what some of the controls did, but he knows I am hopeless with anything mechanical so I just tried to concentrate on what he was saying. He was very pleased with it. And the car was so comfortable to be driven in. I have occasionally been given a lift in some cars which, I have to say, have been very uncomfortable. And they are popular models, too. I am sure they are very good for the driver or for economy, but they are no fun if you are a passenger in the passenger seat or in the back seat!

Of all the cars Barry has ever had, I would say that only the Lexus beats it for comfort and luxury. The Saab was incredibly spacious, and the boot was enormous! We would never have any problems packing for holidays with a boot of that size, and with the expected arrival of another member of the Squit family, that was good news.

David had not gone to bed yet, although he was in his

pyjamas, so there was only one thing to do, and that was lock the doors and go out for a quick drive to Marlborough and back. It seemed like we were in a very prestigious big car. It purred along the A4, making light of any other cars who were pootling along. I had to remind Barry that we had a young one in the back of the car, without a car seat, even if the Saab did have a reputation for being among the world's safest cars! It seemed to me that Barry hardly moved his hands while he was driving. He said it was incredibly easy and hassle-free to drive. I thought it might have been an automatic, but it wasn't. We made sure that having gone through Marlborough town centre to the point of the church and turned round again, that we drove home at a more leisurely pace. David could then be soothed to sleep by the motion of the car and go straight off to his bed when we got home. Barry and I could then have a chat about the day's events, as was our wont.

Barry was clearly delighted with his new car. Better news to come was that the car would be changed at least every two years, and if he ever wanted to buy the car off BAD, he would get it at substantially less than the book value. As it turned out, we didn't keep the 1991 SAAB, but we did keep a later model and it's been kept at the house in Wells ready for when David takes his driving test, hopefully within the next year.

You can imagine the interest that some of the neighbours took in the new car. They were very impressed, and reasoned that Barry must be very important…which, of course, he is. David, our herb-propagating neighbour, thought that the car was "neat". He offered Barry a celebratory 'cigarette', proudly stipulating that they it was hand-made and home-grown by him. Barry felt obliged to take it, but I hope he never smoked it! One of the safest cars on the market, David told him, which of course, by then, Barry and I already knew. Massive boot for all the kit if we ever needed to take it to a gig! (I don't remember discussing Barry's former music career with David, nor does Barry, so we were a bit mystified by that observation.) And we could fit at least five WI members in there if we ever got fed up with Edna's 'carryings on'! I don't think David realised that we got on very well with Edna, or that I was involved with the WI, so I tried diplomatically to suggest that such a comment was a little harsh considering how kind Edna was to a lot of local people. I can't remember his response to that, and despite his little scuffle with the law, I think David was a good sort deep down; it was probably just a little deeper down than the ordinary depth.

I've never really taken a huge amount of interest in cars, to be honest. I do my best whenever Barry gets a new car, but I'm afraid I can't grasp all the technical specifications; they don't appeal to me. As long as the car is a nice colour, comfortable on journeys, and looks quite nice, I am happy. However, it does come in useful sometimes if one is discussing driving safely with one's fellow-members of clubs or associations.

Which brings me nicely to another good event. Lots of good things happened in 1991, although we did have one major disappointment in not being able to get David into nursery in the September (a very feeble excuse was offered, which I don't want to discuss here). Not only did Barry get a great new job, and I fell pregnant, and we got a new car, I was also approached by an acquaintance of one of the WI ladies to join the West Berkshire Conservative Association. And that was to be the start of a long-term association with the Conservatives which continues to this present day.

CHAPTER 18

THE CONSERVATIVE CLUB

Mrs Edwards, who serves with me on one of the sub-committees in our local Conservative branch, ticked me off the other day for calling it a club. It is an Association! So, sorry Mrs Edwards, but, much as I am proud to keep the blue flag flying, I am not that proud! Having been approached to join the Conservatives locally, I was not really sure what to expect. As it turned out, for me it felt like a variation on the WI but with more political and less practical content.

I've got a feeling that the well-to-do lady who introduced me to the Conservatives was called Felicity. I don't really remember too much about her, but Edna thought it would be another string to my bow, and a good opportunity to build up my network of acquaintances. Mum thought so too, although, politically, we don't see entirely eye-to-eye. Mum has socialist links from her past, but tends to categorise herself as in "the middle way" and more of a Liberal. I'll have to be careful not to make too many sweeping comments because I don't want to turn this into my own "little blue book".

Sure enough, there was a very pleasant social aspect to it, but with a young child and being 'in the family way', I was hardly in a position to join in with each social event. When it comes to playing cards, I could play a useful game of knockout whist and rummy, but "bridge" was a complete mystery to me, so I never went to any of the "drives". A few times, Barry and I went on the outings to the canal and left David in the capable hands of Edna. I think the subject-matter of our conversations, however, were terribly dull for Barry, the result being that the only other time Barry has attended one of the Conservatives' functions was a charity ball some years ago.

Barry and I rarely talk about politics, although he knows my views on a number of matters like education, crime and punishment, public transport and the like. Generally, however, what we did agree on was that all governments should not try to nanny us because most of us are capable of making our own decisions. Sadly, as we have got older, we have seen more and more regulation and red tape unfortunately suffocating businesses and interfering with our day-to-day living. One thing that really annoys me – and I'll nail my colours to the mast here and say it - is how stupid it is that new buildings have such lowly placed light switches; it might be okay if you are confined to a wheelchair, but for the 97% of us who move or shuffle around, we don't really want to lean down and wrench our backs trying to turn the light on! I mean, for crying out loud!

Anyway, back to where we were. The folks who attended the various meetings that I went to were perfectly pleasant. I was not really in a position to play a particularly active part, but it was good grounding for my later involvement. If anything, it dispelled the mysticism surrounding what was involved in belonging to a political party. It is so hard to maintain a detached view, but I felt in some ways the Conservative Club (sorry, Mrs Edwards) was probably a variation on the Working Mens Club, or even youth club, or any other association of people with some common interest. Just like them, they would do fund-raising and have social events, but the common interest which bound us was an allegiance to Conservative principles. And I gather the bar was subsidised, which probably ensured frequent attendance by a number of loyal supporters…of subsidised alcohol.

What ensured my interest in politics was a particularly rousing talk on free enterprise by someone we will call William St John Bartholomew. I won't give his real name because he has subsequently been disgraced and has left the party. At the time, I remember being very impressed by him, not just his oratory but also his breadth of knowledge of British industrial history and global factors influencing British trade. (I think Barry would make an excellent politician because he is so clever, but he has always had quite a jaundiced view of British politics so it's very unlikely that you will ever have the opportunity to benefit from his industrial expertise and knowledge.) The only other time I've really been impressed by someone's breadth of knowledge of industrial history was by a well-known industrialist who gave one of the Dimbleby lectures on television some years ago.

Joining the Conservatives was a landmark in my life. I think it gave me some sense of belonging for the first time. I know folks get that when they are involved in a football club or perhaps in church, but for me it was a new experience. I am quite passionate about my association with the Conservatives, but for now I'll leave at that or I'll jump ahead too far.

CHAPTER 19

WELCOME, DANIEL!

You can guage though that 1991 was a very busy year indeed. We were settled into village life and I was getting a bigger tummy in readiness for a special delivery in the January. Barry had a few foreign trips not of any great duration, but he did succeed in his Nigerian trip, negotiating an excellent deal for BAD, the reward for which was an excellent bonus at Christmas-time. I had wanted to order another hamper from Harrods since the last time we had done so was several years back. Barry indicated, however, that he thought our days of ordering hampers from Harrods would be postponed for some years yet.

David enjoyed playing with his toy guitar and continued to be a chirpy soul. With Barry working long hours, it was quite tiring looking after David and carrying a child, but those of you ladies who have had more than one child will know that anyway. Sorry. It's very difficult not to get tetchy when you are tired, so on more than one occasion both David and Barry got the wrong end of a mood swing! Barry is generally quite placid, so he took it in his stride. David, however, is a little more sensitive, and I think he sensed something strange was happening and felt a little threatened.

It was a relief, therefore, to get to the hospital and get on with the task of giving birth. Working on previous experience, and having liaised with the health visitor attached to the local medical centre, we had agreed that I would ensure that Barry was close to hand so that when my waters broke, I could at least get to Newbury Community Hospital promptly. Daniel was due on the January 3rd so it was fortunately close to the start of the year before businesses take off again after the Christmas holidays. Barry was able to get home at a reasonable time on the 3rd but nothing happened. We went to bed, naively expecting to get a good night's sleep ready for what the 4th would bring, only to be disturbed at about 2 a.m. by when I experienced a strange whooshing sensation. It was time!

Mum was staying with us, so Barry quickly tipped her off that it looked like today was the day, and then we got ourselves into the car, the passenger seat pre-prepared with a nice thick, fluffy towel, and my overnight bag ready in the rear of the car. Barry started to drive very fast, which was very unsettling even in my pregnant state. I assured him that the only way the baby was likely to be born in less than the speed it would take us to get to the hospital was a as a result of shock. There then ensued a more enjoyable journey.

By 3.15 a.m. I was safely under the watchful eyes of the midwife on duty in the maternity ward. The contractions were becoming more frequent, and by five o'clock, it was all happening. I won't bore you with all the details. Suffice to say that at 5.52 a.m. we were the proud parents of Daniel Anthony Squit, a healthy eight pound baby boy, supporting his very own pseudo-Mohican hairstyle!

What a fidget he was! We should have known the young fellow was going to be one of those children who are always on-the-go, interested in everything, and full of limitless energy. How fortunate we are that it turned out for us that come bedtime, he switched off and went into a sound sleep when he was a little older or we would be completely frazzled! Daniel is such a clever thing, like his father, Barry.

Everything worked out really well that day. The midwifery team wanted to keep Daniel and me in just for the day, but if all was well they said we could go home the following morning. That meant that after the tidying up that has to happen after birthing, and once everything was settled down, Barry was able to go home, have a wash and brush up and get himself off to work for the day.

Having given mum the update on how long the baby was and what he weighed, and what was his name (she had already worked out it was a boy!), and no he didn't have jaundice, Barry checked up on David and how he was with all the comings and goings. As far as David was concerned, Barry had just popped in to say 'hello'. He was oblivious to the fact that his daddy had been up most of the night with mummy waiting for little David's brother to arrive. Apparently, he merely asked his daddy, "When will I see my brother?" and "Will he look small and smell?" Children come out with the funniest question, don't they?

Mum was happy to look after David, who kept her amused with various renditions of nursery rhymes, apparently confusing the familiar tunes so that the most bizarre and imaginative lyrical arrangements came out such as 'Jack and Jill' to the tune of 'Old Macdonald had a farm'. I've no idea how he accomplished it, but it reinforces my conviction that David was gifted with a love for music from a very early age.

Mum took a call that day from the vicar, who was asking how I was and whether I'd had the baby, and would I like him to visit me in hospital. The kind offer was declined, especially as the plan was for me to come home the following day. Also, Edna popped round to see whether there was any news, and expressed her delight when she heard that there would be another little boy for her to baby-sit.

Mum and Edna got on very well thankfully, maybe because they were a similar age and had broadly similar upbringings and outlook on life. Mum bore no animosity or jealousy towards Edna, despite the obvious fact that David was very comfortable having either Edna's or mum's attention and would swap between laps. It's nice when that happens, isn't it, instead of petty jealousy and having tension in the air.

Barry worked a relatively short day in the office. No doubt he brought some work home - he often did – but it meant that he could pop in to the hospital early that evening and see how young Daniel and I were faring. Very well. Daniel took to feeding as if he had already studied and fully understood the manual whilst inside my womb. Wonderful! It made the day so enjoyable; I was quite relaxed. I even managed to read a few chapters of my book between resting and feeding. (I can't remember what the book was. Probably something light and uninspiring. Better not mention any authors; I might get sued!)

Having enough to keep himself busy the following day for working from home, Barry arrived at the hospital to collect Daniel and me at eight o'clock the following morning. I had been awake a long time. No chance to rest when the early morning vacuuming of the hospital floors is commenced. It also gave me a chance to get free of daytime television. Ugh! Ghastly! What absolute drivel they put on, don't they? I think the only thing I like about it is the little jingle that introduces the programme. Why can't they put on the radio at a low, unobtrusive volume? Then again, I suppose music and radio presenters are liked only according to one's taste so hospitals are unlikely to keep everyone happy no matter what entertainment medium they select.

Waiting for me when I got home were not only a happy mum and David, but also the most gorgeous bouquet of flowers – or, rather, bouquets. Mum had taken time to put the roses in two vases, leaving the other bouquet for me to observe and handle and smell before she dealt with it in similar fashion. I think there was a lovely mix of lilies and irises. It felt so good to be in my own home with family. Two children now. That was wonderful. David now had his own brother. We had two sons. Mum had two grandsons. Children! I said a quiet little prayer of thanks for these gifts.

David kept having a curious look at Daniel in his cradle. Mmm. It was a proper person, not a pretend one like a doll or toy he had seen in Sunday school or mums and tots. It was so funny. I watched him leaning over and smelling his brother, and tentatively reaching his hand slowly towards his brother's little face and then his little hands. Very sensitive. I think David's always been sensitive. Wouldn't it be fascinating to hear what goes on in the mind of a very young child, say less than three years old, when a sibling is first presented to them?

I think David was less than impressed when he realised that his lovely, adorable brother had astounding lung capacity when it came to expressing his hunger! The worried look on his face soon turned to a frown, and I suspected that one of our battles might be with jealousy as David would receive less attention now that there was someone else to vie with mummy and daddy for it.

CHAPTER 20

OUR LOVELY BOYS

Young Daniel, I recall, had a simply staggering appetite almost from the moment he was born. I've already stated that I think David has a very sensitive side, but seeing his younger brother constantly feeding off me, and with his strange little Mohican quiff, must have deeply unsettled him. Many people have since said to me that where the age gap between the first and the second child is about eighteen months or more, jealousy does creep in with the firstborn because, naturally, they do not receive as much attention as they previously would have done. That may be so, but David continued to show an interest in his younger brother and was very careful when touching him. He certainly didn't try to scratch his face or hit him, which I gather some siblings attempt. Terrible really, isn't it?

Daniel piled on the weight and became a bit of a cherub with his rather inflated rosy-cheeked face and rotund little body. Mum thought he was a little angel. Daniel occasionally yelled when he was very hungry, but he was such a good little boy. I think he slept through the night from about three weeks old, so we were very fortunate indeed.

Some of the mums who attended Sunday morning worship in the big village church had organised among themselves a type of informal "mums and tots" group which rotated round a few houses in the village. I wasn't a leader as such, not at that point, but we had a very big living room so we were able to act as hosts on a regular basis. Shirley, who had three young children – none of them as young as Daniel – also hosted these gatherings. I remember even then that she was quite a big lady, younger than me, long straight hair – and that was before the days of GHD hair straighteners! A very matter-of-fact young lady, you could probably best describe her as a bit of a rough diamond. She lived in a reasonable sized property with a good long garden. I think the property belonged, or had belonged, to the local council at some point. Never mind the fact that Daniel had only just been born, it was a case of "onwards and upwards", and when I had not turned up to the gathering the Wednesday after his birth, she phoned to remind me "tots group" had resumed and hoped to see all of us the following week.

David loved these "tots group" gatherings. We were so disappointed that we could not get him into the local private nursery; I think it would have made such a difference to his education. I often wonder whether he might have fared stronger academically if he had started nursery earlier, but I'm sure it's all turned out for the best. After all, he has excellent social skills and the most bizarre and incomprehensible sense of humour; plus, he is very creative. David writes the lyrics for the band's songs and he has written quite a bit of poetry (not that I have seen much of it). I think he may also have written some short books. (He won't let me see them because, he says, I won't "get it".)

At least in "tots" he could play with toys and move about freely without having to stay sitting still and learning early discipline. He loved it when we got the paints out and the big pieces of A3 paper. What a mess! Thankfully, Shirley and the other mums were not so rigid as to miss the funny side of bits of liquid paint ending up on their sleeves or on the carpet or the arms of the chairs. I must admit, I always made a point of having a big sheet on the floor if we ever used paints in our living room. That's the problem if you have a cream coloured carpet. The good thing is that the paints were all water-based! The kids loved doing all sorts of strange compositions which, these days, if someone more well-known were to do it, would probably be sold for silly money to an art gallery, and maybe even to the Tate!

Jigsaws! No, I'm not about to say that Daniel began doing jigsaws in the spring of 1992, but David, his brother, was astonishingly determined in tackling jigsaws. They are very good for developing strategic thinking, in my opinion. What do you start with? All the edges? Do you then look at the picture on the box for a definite object and pick out all the pieces which look like part of the object. David started to do the fifty-piece jigsaws in tots (I'm not going to keep putting it in quotes. It gets tedious after a while, doesn't it?), and when I saw how well he was doing, it stimulated my own former interest in completing jigsaw puzzles. I found some old 1000-piece jigsaws and bought a big piece of ply-board so that I had a decent surface to lay the pieces on when I started doing them. In addition to that, I had to invest in some more jigsaws to accommodate David's new interest. Sometimes Barry was able to join in, and you know how addictive they can be once you find a few pieces and can see the puzzle taking shape.

Often, I would put Daniel in the little rocker near to where

David would be working on a 250-piece or larger jigsaw. In between gurgling and shoving his fingers in his mouth, he would watch attentively his brother attempting to bring together the various objects in the puzzle to create the whole, David being a picture of concentration. He is fortunate not to have a furrowed brow already, thinking back to how much he would frown and crease his forehead when attempting these puzzles.

Edna thought our two boys were delightful and was thrilled with any opportunity to baby-sit. She had such wonderful patience and an unquenchable interest in children and the wonderful ways in which they develop their intelligence and their personalities. Little Daniel soon grew to like this dear lady whom we saw at least twice a week.

Having the two young boys meant I was not as regular in attending WI meetings, but that posed no difficulty for Edna. And as for my involvement in the Conservatives, that had to take a temporary back-seat.

We made sure we pre-booked a place for Daniel in the local private nursery, "See-Saws" (funny name, but easy to remember, so probably good for any marketing they did), so that there would be no problem in him being admitted in the September of 1994 or earlier if they would take him. Sometimes, See-Saws would admit children in the spring if they were either potty-trained or left their nappies in place and could demonstrate a modicum of responsiveness to extra-parental discipline. I certainly hoped the latter would be the case, and that maybe if David was going to start there in the September it would also count in our favour.

Having missed a number of church services after Daniel's birth, I thought I should get back into the routine of going. It was good for the children to mix with a range of ages, and there are usually all sorts of people in any church, and all ages. The vicar and his wife were friendly and made us feel welcome and not guilty when we resumed attending services of worship in the March. Had we thought of christening Daniel? David wasn't christened, so I said it had not really passed through my mind, although I was thankful to God for the gifts of our lovely boys. We agreed that I would talk it over with Barry and let him know in due course.

Daniel was a healthy little boy and always passed with flying colours any check-ups we had with the local health visitor. Other than minor mastitis, I had no problems and was relieved to see my bump almost reverting to normal, not that I can say the same thing about the tyre-marks which encircled my waist!

Easter came and went. The weather was so good late April that we even managed to enjoy a bar-b-q one Saturday evening.

I'm sure David thought that was great fun, standing with his daddy whilst he turned over a mix of sausages, wonderful proper beefburgers from a local butcher, and chicken thighs. Some of the neighbours had brought the usual salads. Shirley turned up with her entourage. Edna was there, along with some of the WI ladies. Barry and I have never been particularly big drinkers, but that did not stop some of our guests turning up with large quantities of lager! Fortunately, no-one disgraced themselves, and Barry must have been good or I would have remembered it surely. It was a great social occasion.

And another social occasion needed to be organised before I completely forgot about it!

CHAPTER 21

THE CHRISTENINGS

Barry, I have to say, was not overly enamoured when at the start of May I finally remembered to mention christenings to him. It's not that he didn't believe; he felt that the whole christening set-up was strange given that both David and Daniel were far too young to express any religious opinion or to have faith. I disagreed with him as regards David. I thought that David was quite capable of expressing faith. It certainly didn't have to be complicated or deeply thought through, and what was wrong with childlike faith? In any event, I explained that it was not so much the children as us committing to bring the children up according to Christian principles and not to keep them away from the church.

Put like that, Barry said that we were doing that anyway so what was the point of christening? I thought it wouldn't do any harm, and if we were already doing what we would be asked to commit to, at least we could keep our promise. When mum and I discussed it, she was fairly relaxed, saying that we wouldn't be able to make David and Daniel believe; they would have to make up their own minds, but certainly it wasn't a bad thing.

I met up with the vicar following one of the services in early May to discuss further the christening of Daniel and asked whether David could be 'done' at the same time. He was delighted. However, the earliest date the vicar could fit us in (sounds very formal, doesn't it?) was the third Sunday in June. He was very enthused because there were two other christenings being done, so he would get to do four in one service. That would be great cause for celebration with these new lives being welcomed into the church. I wasn't asking to become a fully paid-up member of the Church of England, but I didn't want to dampen his enthusiasm. Even more so if I were to confess to being more of a non-conformist, preferring their more informal style of worship! I dread to think how that would have gone down, although I suppose if he had been out in Africa, he'd probably seen a lot more varieties of worship than I ever would.

I am conscious that I haven't told you his name yet. It's

strange, but I feel duty-bound to introduce you, even though you will probably never meet him. He must be in his early seventies by now. He was one of those folks who you probably thought was older than he really was just by virtue of his life experience. Maybe I used to be more judgmental in the past, but I had presumed he would have a very refined, aristocratic-sounding name. I couldn't have been more wrong. Andrew and Cynthia Jones. Cynthia, his wife, was very well-spoken and a very caring person. To many she would have seemed well-to-do and upper class but she was a truly lovely lady. Andrew, although being well-spoken, definitely had a strong sense of humour and, as I have previously mentioned, made a real effort to get alongside the children.

I think this lovely couple had struggled to be accepted in the village because the previous incumbent was regarded with such high esteem almost to the point of veneration. It seems to me that if he had been a Catholic he would have been a saint by now, by all accounts! Whereas, it seemed to me that the parishioners overlooked the reality that Andrew genuinely tried hard to care for his parishioners and to make himself available. I don't think he was particularly impressed by big pompous ceremonies. In my subsequent visits to other Anglican churches, I have often heard the vicar effuse about some big confirmation service or major gathering happening at the cathedral, or the Bishop is doing whatever, and everybody should go along. I went fairly regularly to the church but I don't recall Andrew ever promoting any of that sort of thing. Maybe some of his parishioners expected him to be a typical vicar and do whatever the previous chap had done. In a slightly unusual way, Andrew was, I suspect, his own man. The only thing I really objected to was one service where he came into the service from a side-room wearing this most ridiculous outfit that made him look like a member of the Ku-Klux Klan. No doubt someone will tell me it means something, but – please! – it looks positively awful! We had quite a chuckle about it afterwards and Andrew saw the point I was making. After all, what if Barry wanted to bring one of his black acquaintances or a colleague from the "deep south" in America along to a church service?

Having settled on mid-June for the christenings, I was pleasantly surprised when Andrew asked me if either Barry or I would like to choose any hymn or Christian song for the service. I think many of us are familiar with "All things bright and beautiful", and "He who would valiant be", or "Praise my soul, the King of Heaven", but it is so easy to be over-familiar and miss out the meaning of words. So, I asked him whether he knew the song about "Wide, wide as the ocean". Not a problem. I don't know where he heard it; I thought they only sang it in non-conformist churches but I wasn't about to say that to him. (I hasten to add that we have since had many excellent discussions and I am happy to acknowledge that Andrew has been a great help to me with the spiritual side of my life.) When Barry suggested to Andrew playing "Man on the silver mountain" by Rainbow, he saw the funny side of it, and teased Barry whether he wanted to share after the song was played why it meant so much to him. There was no rock music played in the service.

Mum stayed with us that weekend. Edna got herself all geared up, finding the most amazing hat in one of the posher shops in Marlborough. Barry was in a quandary over whether he should wear a suit or smart trousers and jacket. I found an old dress suit I hadn't worn for a few years, so I suppose I was very fortunate that I was able to fit in it. I'm not a big fan of hats, so that was one less expense to think of. Anyway, the purpose of the service, I reasoned, was to say thank you to God publicly for the gift of our two lovely boys, and to commit to bringing them up in the Christian way, not to win a fashion parade!

You should have seen Shirley. I don't think I will ever forget it. She was, as I mentioned, rather a big lady. She opted to put on these very high-heeled shoes, a very dark skirt which stopped some six inches short of her knees, and a very tight fitting white cotton shirt. The buttons were positively crying out to break free! She also had this strange burgundy jacket where the sleeves ended in line with her elbow. Gorgeous colour, but the overall image definitely made an impression. You could see a number of the menfolk at the service totally captivated, or entranced – one or the other – by her attire. Even Bob, the local builder, was there to witness the occasion.

Andrew, I am grateful to say, was not wearing his Klan outfit that day, but had opted for plain charcoal grey shirt with the dog-collar and smart black trousers. It was a lovely service. David was rather bemused by the christening itself when Andrew got hold of the christening beaker and poured water over his head. Little Daniel's eyes suddenly protruded as if to exclaim, "What d'you do that for?!", at the moment he was christened, and then he was okay. At the point where the vicar anoints each child with olive oil and says "Christ claims you for His own", I think David was getting very irritated. He started to cling to me, worried about what else was the vicar going to do, and when was I going to protect him? I think the parents of each of the other children who were baptised got away quite lightly because each child was only about three or four months old, and most of the time they were asleep. The children that is!

After the service, we had arranged to have a bar-b-q in our garden. We did not know what the other families had organised, so they were invited, but because they had invited many of their relatives and friends, they had already arranged parties. We had a great time. We had beer and lager left over from our previous bar-b-q, so there was plenty of drink available for those who felt they wanted to 'wet the baby's head'. Andrew and Cynthia came back to our house, accompanied by Bob, apologising that they had to make a brief appearance at each of the other parties first, but once they had done that, they were able to relax and enjoy a very companionable and relaxed afternoon with the few folks who had gathered with Shirley, Edna, mum and a small number of other select invitees. We had such a shock when Andrew looked us in the eye and asked, "You have met my brother, Bob, haven't you?" You could have knocked me down with a feather; I was so surprised. And then, upon reflection, I thought why shouldn't the vicar have a brother who was not in the church ministry? Bob himself was not given to using bad language and was a very good worker, that couldn't be denied. Andrew detected my surprise and emitted a loud belly laugh. "It's all right, Sylvia. He's on the right side; he just can't afford the kit." I thought that was a little irreverent, but it showed me that Andrew had the ability to laugh at himself. Bob, it turned out, had actually served God as a missionary in a children's orphanage in Brazil in the 1970's. Wow! It's amazing what 'comes out of the woodwork', I thought. You can imagine some of the discussion we had during the course of the afternoon and early evening. Absolutely fascinating, I can assure you.

Mum and I agreed it was a day of celebration. Barry was slightly more cynical but conceded that it was an enjoyable day, helped by lovely weather and what he called "relatively easy" company.

I asked David quite recently whether he remembered the day of his christening. I got a disgruntled, "No".

CHAPTER 22

DAVID STARTS NURSERY

Barry had a number of projects with BAD that kept him occupied during the summer, although it did not prevent him taking some time off to enjoy his young family. We went for some lovely drives around the area in the SAAB. After all, there is so much to explore in Berkshire, Wiltshire, Hampshire and Dorset, all of which are within a fairly easy drive. Some of our trips took in Savernake Forest, Stonehenge, Woodhenge, Ringwood, Hengistbury Head, Christchurch, Devizes and Salisbury plain, as well as the various white horses around the area. Savernake was great because it was so near and we could book a pitch and have a family bar-b-q there. It also meant David could wander around and explore - either with us or within eyeshot of us - and appreciate the grandeur, mystery and antiquity of the old trees of the forest.

After the summer, things would really take off. Daniel was already a capable crawler and at this rate he would be walking well before his first birthday. David was due to start nursery at See-Saws in early September. Barry had another trip to Nigeria planned in October, but there was also a possibility of going to Nicaragua and or Paraguay, and that sounded very exciting. Geography was never one of my strongest subjects, so I tried to listen hard when Barry explained that both countries struggled with rampant inflation and terrible crime rates. Both countries are big coffee and cotton producers, so at least I learned something from Barry's opportunities.

The first week of September arrived, and on the Thursday I was feeling a little tense about David going off to nursery for an 8.30 start. Fortunately, there was no need at this stage in David's education to sort out uniform. That would prevent him becoming unsettled as we walked along to the nursery. Also, it was such a blessing to be able to go and collect him from nursery at lunch-times in the first month. From October, the nursery's policy was that all children should be left for the whole day until finishing time, which was 3 o'clock. The head of the nursery, Mrs Fellingham or Fullingham. (I can't remember so I'll call her Mrs Fellingham for now.) She was a very strong-minded matronly kind of lady, the sort who no doubt has an inbuilt capacity to deal out withering looks on demand without her supply ever running low. The ground rules included no bullying of other children (that was a comfort from my perspective; I didn't anticipate my sensitive David doing that), toilet-trained by age three or the child's place at the nursery would be suspended until compliance; no bad language from any child would be tolerated (I don't know why they expected such young children to have a propensity for that); children should not be sent to nursery on days when they had stomache upsets or obvious colds or the parents would be contacted and requested to collect them. So you can see, it was quite a strict regime. However, it worked both ways. You knew that your child's education and development would not be interrupted by a poor, unfortunate child projectile vomitting on them whilst they were at play and that they would not finish the day in a state of bewilderment because of bullying or general nastiness.

When I collected David at lunch-time, I don't recall that he seemed phased by the experience of being in a different learning environment to our tots gatherings. Daniel was pleased to see him. The afternoon seemed to go off without any difficulties either. Only at the end of the Friday, after his first two days at nursery, did I receive any kind of feedback from the head. David was very quiet and was not particularly forthcoming within the group. That threw me. As far as I was concerned, David had good social skills and was used to mixing with a range of age groups. The oldest child in his group, I presumed, was three. It turned out, however, that the children were of mixed ages, the youngest being slightly older than two, the oldest being four and a half years old.

Given that a child's speech develops at the pace in which it is stimulated, and their ability to deal with various tasks or challenges develops likewise, it seemed to me that David was thrown by the inability of some of the other children and that he had to adjust to some of their slow pace. It transpires that one of the group exercises was to complete a one hundred piece jigsaw. I explained to Mrs Fellingham that David was used to tackling five hundred piece jigsaws because he had been doing them for over a year. After attempting a withering look on me, which I returned with a similarly striking frown (15-all, game on!), I suggested that children developed at different speeds and maybe there was a case for re-thinking some of the group activities. In fairness to her, we didn't experience any further problems the following week and David settled into nursery very nicely.

At the end of September, all parents of children recently

accepted into the nursery were encouraged to attend what was called "First month review". In a very businesslike way, Mrs Fellingham said that David's objective was to be able to read by the end of June 1993, by which time he would be four years old. Mum and Edna and I often read to David – you do, don't you; it's natural – but we had not, as such, taught him how to read. That was the task of nursery, although I think we certainly helped them and David on the way. Mrs Fellingham was very confident he would achieve it if we all pulled together, and it would ensure that his confidence would not be affected when he joined the main school system.

I enquired what sort of extra curricular activities should we expect to be on the horizon over the next six to nine months so that Barry and I could plan our diaries. In addition to a trip to Savernake Forest for the nursery picnic in May, they would probably look to take the children to Cotswold Wildlife Park probably in the March, but before that the nursery would be putting on a Christmas play in December and all the children would be encouraged to participate. That sounded delightful. What would the play be about, I queried? I was informed that a lot of effort would be put into it, including rehearsals and proper costumes, and usually the local press would be in attendance to take photographs. It would be the traditional Christmas story and it would be videoed. Wow! That was exciting. Let me tell you more…

CHAPTER 23

DAVID STARS AS KING HEROD

See-Saws put a lot of effort into their Christmas productions. Bearing in mind they were a nursery and not a primary or junior school, it would be reasonable to expect them to practise in December and give the children the chance to say one or two lines. Oh no! This had to be *the* Christmas production to beat all previous productions.

Towards the end of October, I was given the whole script so that I could be familiar with it, and so that I could ensure David did his best to learn his lines. The fact that David was not a competent reader yet was irrelevant because he could learn 'parrot fashion' his lines from me! I had yet another clash of opinions with Mrs Fellingham. If she had done this with every parent, we would all know the play back-to-front, off-by-heart, and word-for-word because we would have to play every other character's part other than the one our respective children would be playing! Personally, I was not prepared to do that : for one, I did not want to spoil the fun of seeing how the production unfolded, and, secondly, it was unrealistic to expect young children to remember several lines off-by-heart. It was not the same as a song where the lyrics are all together in one place.

I don't think Mrs Fellingham knew what was coming when she first came across me. This was the first time they had planned to do the play in this way, she admitted, and whilst she agreed it might have perhaps been ambitious, she understood – and acceded! – that perhaps it was a bridge too far for such young ones. Would I be willing to come into rehearsals and perhaps help the children by prompting them and reminding them of their lines from mid-November to the date of production? That sounded great fun to me, so we ended up with a happy compromise. You see, people can be so reasonable if we would only speak our mind. (Barry often tells me, he gets very frustrated at work because junior managers are so scared of being insulted by their peers and by senior managers, they dare not challenge various ideas and projects which get proposed. I think he must be very well respected within BAD because, he tells me, a number of projects have been abandoned when he has explained to the Board and fellow senior managers their commercial weakness and unprofitability, or when he has persuaded the Board to part company with various company customers who have drained the company's resources for no positive returns.)

What with the difference of opinions, I had not read the script or given Mrs Fellingham the opportunity of reminding me what David's part would be. King Herod! So, David was going to be the bad guy and a meanie! That would make the actual performance fun because those who would attend could boo and hiss. Mmm. David wasn't used to that so we would have to make sure he was used to it by doing it in rehearsals. This production would really get my creative juices stimulated.

As far as costumes were concerned, two or three of the parents of children at See-Saws were brilliant seamstresses. One of them ran a very posh dress shop in Marlborough where very few of the dresses were for sale at less than one hundred pounds – even in 1992! My offer to involve mum and her dressmaking skills was gently declined, only because that aspect of the production's planning had been addressed even before the new school year had begun.

The nursery had once been the manse for the village Methodist chapel which had closed many years previously. Not only were the former bedrooms upstairs huge enough to comfortably accommodate a teacher with a class of eight children, but the manse had the most wonderful huge reception room. The plan was to put on the production in here. From November, most of the small tables and chairs were rearranged so that they hugged the walls, freeing up space for acting out the play. The boxes of the usual teaching materials were stored at the back of the room, away from where the children would be acting, in a make-shift cupboard with appropriate rounded rubber edging to protect the children in case, in their excitement, they ran into one of its edges while playing. Also, the crash mats and small climbing apparatus were now being stored safely at the back of the room, although they were easy to pull out and use for the scheduled times of play and exercise.

At least by helping out with the production, it gave me the chance to take a pride in what David was doing in nursery. I think it also helped me to feel that, in some way, I was helping or being a part of what the nursery was trying to achieve or provide to the community.

David thought it was great that I was hanging around nursery.

It probably built up his confidence for the following term when his reading ability developed really well. (He did achieve Mrs Fellingham's objective.) He loved acting the part of bad King Herod. A nice little boy called Wilfred got to act the part of Joseph, and a lovely young girl called Priscilla was to be Mary. Fortunately, no real baby was to be used for the part of Jesus, so it was a case of ensuring a very good quality doll was used. Not only that, we were told that on the day of the production, there would be a special surprise!

You don't come across many Priscillas and Wilfreds these days, do you? The only Priscilla I have come across is one who is mentioned in the New Testament in the Acts of the Apostles. As for Wilfred, other than the war poet, Wilfred Owen, and the actor, Wilfred Hyde-White, I can't think of any. Oh yes! I think there is a chap called Wilf at the Conservative Club in Hungerford; I think he liked his Guinness. Anyway, these two lovely children, slightly older than David, took their parts very well. So innocent and loving; it was beautiful to see them acting out the Christmas story, Wilfred very gently caring for his betrothed as they journeyed to Bethlehem only to be told there was no room anywhere.

There were places for thirty-five children in the nursery. At the time, Mrs Fellingham had limited the number to thirty-two because of a recent staffing issue which she would not be drawn to comment on. Trying to ensure that all the children were involved with the production was quite an achievement on her part and the other teachers' parts, I have to admit. We opted to have five wise men, and four shepherds and seven angels, which helped matters along. By the time we had thrown in some religious leaders of the day, and Bob, the vicar's brother (as a local builder in Bethlehem!), everyone had a part.

Throughout November, we practised the production every Friday morning. It was a good way for the children to begin winding down from their learning as the weekend approached. You could see that the children were enjoying themselves. There were a few songs to learn so that they could be sung at key points in the production: "Silent night"; "While shepherds watched their flocks by night"; and, of course, "Little donkey". By the end of November, they were in their element because they were now able to wear their costumes and take on their characters' parts. Herod had a great flowing burgundy-coloured robe, complete with lining and white imitation fur collar. David really did look regal in that robe. The crown looked a little disappointing, I have to say, but the robe was such a dominant feature that no-one else would notice the rather cardboard-looking crown on David's head. We got all the children to boo whenever David came to front of stage to say his lines about where was the baby to be born and when he could go and visit him. To complement this, we encouraged the teachers and a few of the parents who were coming in to help during rehearsals to cheer every time the wise men came on stage. We wanted some humour. After all, there is nothing pleasant about the fact that Herod authorised the most awful slaughter of so many young children at the time of Jesus' birth.

So, my David got to be the bad guy. The first few times he was booed really unsettled him and he was quite upset. After much explaining that it was pretend and that lots of people would be laughing "on the inside", he was persuaded to carry on. Eventually, David cut a stern figure when he was approached by the wise men asking about the one who was to be born king. All of us were confident it would be a very good production.

Come the day of the actual Christmas production, the room was crammed. The make-shift cupboard, crashmats and tables all had to be removed and put in an upstairs room. Chairs had to be brought from upstairs because eighty people were expected by the time you included parents, the mayor and his wife, the vicar and his wife, the local paper and someone from the local radio station. I hadn't realised that the mayor was coming. That was a surprise. But it wasn't the surprise Mrs Fellingham had meant.

The production was going down a treat. The children were smiling naturally and looking as though they were really enjoying themselves, apart from David who had the appropriate degree of gravitas which you would expect for a nasty king. When Mary and Joseph arrived in Bethlehem, there was a general roar of laughter when Bob announced he would be quite happy to put together some sort of shelter for them, but he was very busy with other customers so it would have to wait til the new year! Then, having found the one innkeeper who could accommodate them in his stable if they were happy to sleep in such smelly surroundings, we were truly started by a genuine loud neighing…or should I say, "ee-aw"ing, as a donkey was led to the front of the room by a youth from the village. What a surprise that was! And then, with perfect timing, the children began to sing "Little donkey".

I still think that is probably the best Christmas production I have ever seen. It was so enjoyable, and everyone present loved it. There was an excellent write-up in the local paper, David drawing very positive reviews from the journalist. Also, the representative of the radio station singled him out, alongside Wilfred and Priscilla, for his excellent performance as Herod. What a great achievement!

CHAPTER 24

DANIEL IS AMAZING

I did not want to detract from David's stellar performance as King Herod in the Christmas production, but at the start of the November Daniel astounded us. He has always been an alert and bright little boy, and was an accomplished crawler from a very early age. One early November Saturday morning, David was out in the garden playing on his plastic run-around thing – it was probably supposed to resemble a tractor – and Barry was engrossed in the Telegraph. Daniel was crawling around, gurgling and occasionally exclaiming various grunts when he patted the back of the paper. Barry dropped it to look at what his little boy wanted, and there he was, standing upright, not leaning on the arm of the chair or a toy!

Barry shouted me straightaway. I may have been putting some washing on or tidying up some dishes, I don't know. The next thing we witnessed was Daniel decided he was going to walk towards the patio doors and see what his brother was doing. He made a few steps and fell face first. Rather than cry, he screwed up his face in a mixture of disappointment and annoyance at his body, as if to say, "I'm not best pleased with you for doing that in front of my mum and dad; now, let's go and see David." Obviously he didn't say that because his speech was not that developed, but you know what I mean.

We were both stunned. November. That would make him only just ten months old! And he is already beginning to walk. What an amazing boy! It was a funny sight seeing our youngest boy waddling about the living room with his hands held forward looking like he was ready to go into some kind of Lionel Blair dance routine. That first day, Barry and I were entranced with amazement watching Daniel walk around the living room. Next, he determinedly headed towards the patio door so that he could go outside and be with his brother. I made sure I stood in front of him as he approached the slightly raised grooves in which the doors were mounted before they slid back. Sure enough, he would have gone face first onto the patio if I had not been there to catch him.

Children are very happy to step forward in a very focused way, aren't they, without being concerned about what might be on the ground for them to trip over. There's a lesson for us in that, I'm sure.

Little by little, Daniel's confidence grew and by the time we got to the Christmas production, he was quite a handful. He certainly was not running, but he was becoming a confident little walker, curious about everything now that he could stand up on his own feet. It certainly made for fun and games in the garden as we had to make sure he avoided sticking every leaf or berry he could find in his mouth. Parents always worry about these things and dread the prospect of turning up to casualty with their child foaming at the mouth because they've either eaten something poisonous or had an allergic reaction to something in the garden or to an insect bite or sting.

We already had a guard around the fireplace and its marble hearth, but come Daniel's first Christmas we were more worried that he would pull the six foot pine tree over on himself. He was into everything, and I don't suppose we made it easier for ourselves by decorating the tree with shiny baubles and colourful wire and dangling chocolates. Most of the latter were gone well before Christmas, but I suspect David had helped himself before we blame that on Daniel.

Mum had not sold the family house in Northamptonshire, but was a regular visitor to Chilton. We had a lovely Christmas together, although it would have been even better if daddy could have been there. She stayed over for Daniel's first birthday which was a fairly quiet occasion. Unfortunately, he had a bit of a cold and was a sleepy-head most of the day, probably because of the syrupy medication he was taking. No doubt it was designed for that purpose!

David went back to nursery on the Wednesday, Daniel's birthday having fallen on a bank holiday Monday. It is hard to believe how quickly children grow up, isn't it? Three and a half, and Daniel already one year old. David made very good progress that term. Mrs Fellingham was very pleased with him and thought that he was beginning to grasp the basics of reading, encouraging us to continue reading as often as possible with him to reinforce the nursery's efforts. Daniel loved to look at picture books and we thought nothing of it, but it was later to prove an excellent stimulus to his educational development and his own reading skills.

All children come out with simple words when they are very young, don't they? Maybe it is instinctive, so that they can get what they want, whether it's food, protection, sleep or something else. But, generally, I would not expect most fourteen month-old children to say words other than perhaps 'Mum', 'Dadda', 'Ta', and perhaps some incomprehensible grunts.

Daniel was genuinely a very inquisitive and attentive child, so I suspect that he listened very carefully to the conversations I would have with David or with Barry, and vice versa. Can you imagine my surprise when one tea-time in March he uttered the words, "Thank you, mummy". Initially, I said, "That's okay, darling", before realising that this was not David speaking but his younger brother. Barry and I glanced at each other, and I remember David laughing. Maybe the look on our faces was funny. Children have a very idiosyncratic sense of humour so it's not always easy to understand what it is that made them laugh. "Sandwizzyuh". We frowned again. He must be mimicking! How remarkable! What a clever little boy!

I had got back into the routine of WI after Daniel's birthday and mentioned Daniel's speaking ability to Edna in the week leading up to the clocks being put forward. I was curious to know whether, in her experience, she had encountered such precocious ability in one so young. To my surprise, Edna said it was relatively common many years ago, but her opinion was that with the advent of radio and television, many parents switched off from either talking to each other or to their children so there was very little for children to mimic until they were older and mixing with children at things like tots or playschool or primary school. (I know it's a long sentence before someone starts wittering about using smaller sentences!)

Once he started, there was no stopping Daniel. Before we knew what was happening, he was chuntering all sorts of words. I presume he must have been talking and playing with David and picking up various words, whether from songs David would sing, or from things he heard us say during the day. It was very amusing in many respects. In other ways it was a little bit strange, because it seemed so unusual, almost as if Daniel was a bit 'old before his time'. He is still a lovely young lad, but these two early developments – his walking and his talking – marked out Daniel as an amazing little boy!

CHAPTER 25

BOYS FIGHTING

Well, boys will be boys, so I am sure you won't be surprised by this chapter's heading. Daniel was – and is – a very determined, strong-minded boy, and didn't he want to make sure David knew it at the earliest opportunity! Poor David, after all his support and protection towards David, he wondered what came over Daniel as Daniel developed in leaps and bounds and headed for his second birthday.

I think we must have been relatively fortunate with David. What we thought we had experienced of the "terrible twos" with him was nothing compared to young Daniel. David certainly had his tantrums and outbreaks of possessiveness, but I don't recall him ever being overly aggressive towards his younger brother or uncontrollable from our point of view as parents. Maybe that's the bliss of a mother's memory? Daniel, however, being such an intelligent little fellow, believed that everything had been put in its place in the house and in the garden exclusively for his benefit.

Being so precocious in his speech and with his walking, it was quite hard not to see the funny side of Daniel struggling with the little strength he had to make David surrender toys, books and jigsaw boxes. David is very patient and placid, and even now he is not what you would call a confrontational person. Anything for a quiet life, I think is his motto. But, there is only so much prodding and snatching that any little boy can take.

David had come back from nursery one week in January, not long after Daniel's second birthday, and I suspect he was tired because he was getting more difficult reading exercises, and also I suspect he was becoming a little frustrated and becoming ready for primary school where he would hopefully have more opportunity to use a field to run around in at playtimes   That was the one disadvantage of See-Saws: the children did not usually go into the back garden of the former manse to run around. All play was supervised indoors. That's not what I would regard as a natural environment for play, would you? …even with the best equipment.

So, it did not bode well for Daniel when David had been wandering around in the garden, looking for signs of life: maybe some snowdrops, or maybe there would be buds on some of the bushes or the trees. He had got on his little bike with its stabilisers when Daniel came up to him and started tugging on his shirt. David withdrew Daniel's hand with a view to continue riding his bike. Daniel was indignant and slapped David on his shoulder. Well, that was it, as far as David was concerned. He may be the older boy but he wasn't about to be slapped without providing what he thought was a suitable response. Sometimes, though, children don't realise their own strength, do they? The next thing I know is that Daniel is on the ground having been given his own slap, courtesy of an aggravated older brother. He screamed and shouted, and then he thought he would have a run at David and give him another slap. By this time, I was by the patio doors, horrified that my lovely boys were fighting each other.

I yelled at the boys to stop fighting, but they must have got into "the zone", I think people call it now, totally focussed on who was going to emerge the victor. It's very difficult to be wise in such situations. I've heard of parents in years gone by who adopted the "Stop it now before I bang your heads together" approach. Sounds very dangerous to me, so I wasn't about to do that. A rather feeble, "Children, please stop doing that", emerged from my lips, but that went unheeded. "Pack it in!" I hollered. They broke off fighting for what must have been two seconds. Daniel looked at his brother. David looked a picture of concentration, his brow furrowed. The next thing, Daniel thought he would get another slap in, and then it was back to fighting each other. I walked up to the two of them to separate them, and then, taking each by the hand, we went into the house. I have to admit, Daniel was dragged in because he thought he would go to ground to avoid coming indoors. There followed a good healthy verbal dressing-down. I knew David was sensitive enough to understand how upset I was. As for Daniel, I was not so sure. Daniel was also too young to understand the concept of "kiss and make up", or shake hands and be friends. I just had to hope. Discussing it with Barry later, he was quite relaxed about the whole incident and said that eventually they would settle down and natural order would take over. It sounded very fatalistic and 'survival of the fittest', which he knew I didn't agree with. I still don't.

Sure enough, within the week, the boys were at it again. This time, it was over a video. I think David must have been watching that strange children's cartoon, Pingu, and Daniel decided that he wanted a different video. (Mmm. I wonder if I could get the makers of Pingu to endorse our family having given them a mention. Maybe SAAB could provide a complementary car! That's an idea, isn't it?) Not the safest place to have a fight, in front of the television and with all the wiring nearby. Children do not always shout and scream when they are fighting though, especially boys. As a parent, you just become aware that it has gone relatively quiet apart from a sense of lots of bumps and grunts and the occasional exclamation of an item of crockery or glassware breaking.

I found the boys' fighting very unsettling. Barry was so relaxed about it, and when I phoned mum to discuss the matter, she also said it was perfectly normal. Fortunately, Edna was nearby. I did not know a lot about her family other than that she had been widowed at the young age of thirty-seven. I don't think I ever saw any relatives come to visit her so I presumed she was childless. As regards the latter presumption I was right, but years ago, before bureaucracy suffocated many willing folks' desire to adopt or foster, she had fostered a number of children. She did not say when she had done so, or whether her husband had been involved while he was alive. However, the fact of the matter, she said, was that I should be very grateful to have two such lovely boys who were completely normal, and that I should be more worried if they did not fight. "If Cain and Abel struggled, why should we be any different?" Edna had a number of interesting maxims, of which this was just one.

The fighting continued up until David was about fifteen by which time Daniel had calmed down tremendously and had calculated that David was physically much stronger than him and would probably win each fight. Having said that, siblings have a natural protective instinct so that, although they are happy to fight with each other, if anyone else fights their sibling they will naturally dive in to support them.

It's so embarrassing though, isn't it, when your children start fighting each other when you have company or when you are in someone else's home or out shopping. That really tested me. I don't particularly agree with hitting children, and certainly wouldn't want to encourage it, but I have to confess that on rare occasions, the boys' fighting whilst we were shopping in town got the better of me and they would each get such a smack on the underside of their thighs. It certainly hasn't scarred them for life and they are perfectly well-adjusted (for all those goody-goodies out there who think that smacking is an abomination. Don't get me started on how we should punish children who use vile language and being unruly!)

Things certainly didn't get any easier when David started primary school in the September. He had turned five in the June and I suspect he felt it was time that little Daniel showed respect to his older brother. Daniel, however, did not appreciate yet the need to show his older brother a little more respect, nor did he realise that it was in his interest to be kind to his brother because he would need his older brother's protection by the time he started primary school. So, I think it is fair to say that we had our share of challenges when the boys were very young.

CHAPTER 26

BARRY'S PROMOTION

Time goes very quickly when your children are very young. With the first child, the first months are traumatic, worrying about every little cough and cry, wondering whether you are being a good enough parent. The months then pass by as you get into the feeding, sleeping and changing routine, and check-ups and being wary about what commitments you take because of what you can do with your baby. Then, before you know it, the first birthday has arrived and you hurtle towards the child's second birthday. By the time the second one is born, the speed of time seems to have accelerated and your own birthday numbers seem to rotate as quick as the digit counter on the electric meter when you have the washing machine, tumble drier and kettle on all at the same time.

Suddenly, I was no longer in my early thirties but was heading towards the infamous special fortieth birthday. There was the prospect of Daniel starting nursery in the new year, Barry was going great guns with his job. Perhaps I shouldn't use that euphemism because I think his company did have a factory somewhere which manufactured and refurbished munitions. Barry mentioned it once when he had imbibed a little too much alcohol but then went on to tell me it was such a small part of the company's operations that I shouldn't worry about it.

Mrs Fellingham at See-Saws was very impressed by our precocious Daniel and agreed that he could start nursery in the January of 1995. He had just turned two. The agreement was that he should only attend in the mornings for the first term and then, after Easter, he could spend the whole day there with the other children. This seemed to be a very good arrangement. I sensed early on that Daniel was something of a child prodigy and that it would only be a short time before he achieved some other astounding feat. Maybe he would be able to read before the end of the year. Or perhaps he would be able to play the piano, or something like that.

Shortly after Daniel had started nursery, around mid-January, Barry came home one night to say that the following day he had an important interview. BAD would be interviewing three senior managers for the role of Head of Operations. It sounded very important. Barry was one of the interviewees. Understandably, he was a little tense, but he was also confident but without being arrogant. He had to do a presentation so I didn't see much of him that night after he had eaten his dinner. So, no guitar playing or reading with David and Daniel.

The following night, Barry returned home quite late. Well, probably not that late, but it always seems late when the days are shorter, doesn't it? The thing was, it was dark when he got home. Both children were in their beds, chuntering away. Did he get the job, I queried? One of three candidates had been told he was unsuccessful, but Barry and the other candidate would find out at the end of the week because the Personnel Department needed to review the benefits of each candidate and assist the Board with a final review of the two remaining candidates' skills and previous performance. From what Barry recalled, the other chap, in his early fifties, had overseen a very successful review of internal processes. Barry didn't say what; he thought I would find it boring and, what with all the technical jargon, it might leave me confused as well. Other than that, he was not aware that the candidate had been involved in negotiating any big deals with major clients nationally or internationally so he felt he was in with a good chance of success.

It was Wednesday so there would be another two days to wait. Barry was rather fond of a glass of Chateauneuf of an evening. Not to pre-judge success, we had a glass of wine together and mused on whether winning a promotion would have any bearing on the family's situation given our experience the last time Barry's job situation changed. We both appreciated that the children were making good progress with their education and that there was a lovely community in the village, work being relatively close for Barry. However, with the boys getting older, and with the hope of adding to the family maybe in the near future, it might make sense to move to a slightly larger house. Ideally, however, it would need to be not too far from Barry's work to ensure that he did not miss out on the children growing up. We certainly would not need to move this year, but we could aim to move during the first quarter of the following year, and that is what we decided on.

I don't think we had a very big mortgage on the Chilton property which, by now, had begun to appreciate in value. Prices were still a little subdued having not fully recovered from the plummeting values of the early nineties. That worked in our favour. If we could find another nice property, we would have the opportunity to consider renting out the Chilton property without selling it. We could also consider having some sort of annex built onto the next property, unless there was one already in situ, so that mum could come and live with us. That is something I had wanted to happen for a long time. Barry was very accommodating as far as that was concerned. I know lots of men would be horrified by the prospect of their mother-in-law living anywhere near them. But then again, Barry is such a wonderful man. Whether we would find somewhere close by or perhaps in Hampshire would remain to be soon. I can't say I was too keen to live anywhere near Reading itself, but that was purely personal preference. I really liked being in a village in the countryside. I thought – and so did Barry – it was much better for the children. The good news was that we had plenty of time to investigate possible locations.

Lunch-time on the Friday, I was about to retrieve Daniel from nursery when something else cried out for my attention – the telephone. It was Barry, talking rather animatedly. Well? Yes! He had been appointed Head of Operations. Excellent news! His salary had been dramatically increased to reflect his new responsibilities (not that Barry is particularly driven by money), and he would get a full time personal assistant, and if he ever needed to attend a business function, he could have his own chauffeur at the company's expense! There was more detail but he had to rush off for a meeting, leaving me to don my coat and rush along to nursery to collect Daniel.

It was a pleasant surprise to see Barry home by six-thirty that night. It meant that not only could he have some fun time with the boys but we could also discuss further what his job involved and what it would mean for the Squits. Although the role to be filled by Barry was Head of Operations, it would also entail him developing the relationships he had already established in Nicaragua (Paraguay had 'bombed out'), Colombia and Venezuela in addition to developing new European relationships. There was a company in Switzerland (N.A.F. Systems) which BAD were very interested in, so Barry would need to visit there on a regular basis with the sweetener that one day he might be required to be based out there. How exciting for us!

Barry had a good knowledge of who the key clients were in the UK as well as how these clients were managed (or "delivered service", as he liked to say). The role would involve many more overseas trips and us being apart more often, but the goal was that with good planning, Barry aimed to retire from full-time employment by the age of fifty-five; earlier, if various aspects of his financial planning came to fruition. Barry has always been clever with money, without being a hoarder, and had hopes of living somewhere very warm when he was a little older: maybe Tenerife or the south of France.

That Friday was definitely an occasion to celebrate. Another bottle of Chateuneuf was uncorked and we both got a little inebriated and raucous, most unusual for me. Edna popped round briefly to pass on some details of forthcoming events at the Conservative Club, which one of the members had dropped off, not having seen much of me for some time. That was nice, I thought. Edna was, I think, slightly bemused to see me looking so flushed and wobbly because of the alcohol, and it did make feel a little naughty.

Edna was like an additional mother to me, keeping an eye on me on behalf of my own mum, so it was no surprise when I had a phone call from my mother the following morning to ask if everything was okay. Mum was delighted with our news. I reassured her that we were not about to abandon her to Northamptonshire but we would probably begin to look for another property, and hopefully it would have an existing annex or enough land to build one for her so that she could live with us. By then, mum was feeling that, being in her mid-seventies, a house the size she was living in, together with the huge garden, was too much of a burden, even though she did employ a gardener four days a week and a housekeeper three days a week.

Shirley, whose youngest child was at nursery with Daniel. (Isn't it terrible, I can't remember her daughter's name!), met me on the Monday morning and we exchanged the usual pleasantries together with my piece of good news. I believe she was genuinely sad at the prospect of us moving away from the village. I think she had found it quite hard to make close friends, and although I wouldn't say we were really close as such, we both felt a warm affection for each other and an interest in each other's well-being. I don't think Shirley had an ounce of jealousy in her body, in spite of how well we were obviously doing as a family. In many respects, Shirley was like a young girl herself, only she was living in a rather well-endowed, large adult body. She was a big softy who loved her children, and was happy to be anywhere near other children. When I collected the children later that day, she met me with a card and a bottle of wine. (I think it was one of those modestly priced fizzy German wines but, nonetheless, it was a nice thought.)

Oh dear! We were only in January and already I sensed we were in the countdown to moving away from the village. We hadn't even looked at any houses yet. I think my mood went up and down throughout January and February, and it only really brightened when Barry proposed one weekend that we go on holiday together as family in late July to somewhere nice and hot, where we could relax in the sun, and the children could swim and play and we could all have fun. It sounded ideal. What was the plan? Tenby? Bournemouth? Torquay? No! Tenerife! Brilliant! That was something to look forward to.

CHAPTER 27

THE SQUITS' FAMILY'S BRILLIANT HOLIDAY

David had begun primary school in the village in September of the previous year and made gradual progress. His success in grasping the basics of reading at See-Saws proved to be a great help as he settled into mainstream education. I respected Mrs Fellingham's business-like approach in setting one or two objectives for each child for each year they were in attendance. I thought that was a good thing.

It is a pity that once the children settle into bigger schools, many of them struggle to cope with the individual school's education philosophy or teaching methods. We do not all learn in the same way, and most of us throughout life resent being viewed as a number or someone who is making up the numbers. We had opted not to send David to a private school because we knew some of the little ones from See-Saws would be going to the local primary school, and we considered that was the healthier option for David. Besides, the school had a growing reputation for high standards.

I think if David had not been such an able reader he would have been overwhelmed by primary school. He was desperate to play games outside and to be creative, but with the bias towards academic achievement and league tables, I believe he became a little frustrated and it affected his behaviour. I was so surprised to be informed by his teacher just before Christmas that David had a tendency to be disruptive in class and to "goon around" when he should have been concentrating. He seemed to enjoy other children's attention by being silly and it was something we needed to help the school address in a positive way. There was no Christmas production to look forward to. Rather, the school were thinking of putting on a simple, shorter version of "Joseph and the amazing technicolour dreamcoat" next spring, so the head of year and I agreed that this was something we should perhaps look towards to help David improve his behaviour. I explained that David loved singing, so maybe he could have one of the main singing parts. We left that in abeyance for the time being without any assurances from David's teachers.

Daniel flew past his third birthday and was proving an astounding pupil at See-Saws. For Mrs Fellingham, he was her star pupil. Academically brilliant, responsive to any mental stimulus, he constantly exceeded her targets. By his third birthday, he could read simple books unaccompanied, and then show the books to the nursery teachers and tell them the story. Some children like to read the same book again and again. Apart from the book about the hungry caterpillar, and the Roald Dahl book about the giant peach, Daniel thirsted for new material. He showed very little interest in jigsaws, so I wondered if he would be one of these very academic children who have an amazing ability to store huge quantities of information without majoring on the creative side. Subsequently, Daniel has proved that he has his aesthetic side, learning piano and violin (he dropped piano) and it wasn't so long ago he wrote an article for our very first Christmas Niseletter (January 2005). You do worry sometimes, don't you, if your children are exceptionally intelligent, will they fail to appreciate the wonders of their surroundings and neglect to get in touch with what you hope are their natural sensitivies?

At school, David was able to use a computer. The school had invested a considerable amount of money in lots of computers and there was a real drive to ensure that the children were at ease with using this new technology and not in any way fazed by it. Now, if Mrs Fellingham had been there, I'm sure she would have told us that David's objective for the first year would be to study certain computer games and get to what she would consider an appropriate level which tested his strategy, planning and execution skills.

The school's loss was See-Saws' – and therefore Daniel's – gain. At home, we did not have a computer, although sometimes Barry brought home something he called a "lap-top", a portable computer which he would take off into the spare room to work on his many projects. With the lap-top, Barry was able to go on the "world wide web", some ex-military creation which enabled people to store information centrally on a "website" and to communicate with each other by electronic mail through the medium of a modem (whatever one of those is!) using the telephone socket. Barry told me that this was the age of the information super-highway. Of course, the only thing you can do when someone utters something totally incomprehensible is to nod sympathetically and appear to show interest. I had heard one or two mums mention "email" but can't claim to have understood what they meant at the time.

Apparently, this was not just the way to find information about all sorts of subjects, but also was the way to book holidays and find special offers, so Barry assured me. For me, the end product was more important. Therefore, I was pleased when he told me that the holiday had been booked in a very nice hotel in Tenerife, equipped with swimming pool, private gardens, and a short walk from the beach. And Barry had negotiated a very good price for us because he is very clever like that.

By the time our holiday came round, Daniel was three and a half and David had just had his sixth birthday. Barry had never expressed a great deal of interest in football, whether it be to watch it on the television or to go and watch a match or to play the game. I think David found this a little frustrating when he joined primary school because many of the other boys loved to play football and clearly came from homes where football was *the* sport to follow, some of them having their favourite football team's shirt with their favourite player's number and name. He loved to run around with the ball, tackling and shooting, and was very keen to get into a football team. Sometimes, David would invite two or three of his school friends back after school, or they would come round on a Saturday morning, and play a game of football together. Occasionally, David would go in goal and pretend he was the hero making brilliant saves, just like he had seen on some of the television programmes on Saturday lunch time.

It soon became obvious that he had found another passion to go with his singing. The only time the village team seemed to play was on a Sunday when we went to church, which I thought should take priority over football, so we held off him joining that team. Regularly after school, he and a number of school friends would go to the local 'rec' and kick a ball about until it was tea-time. The number of times he would come back with grass stains on his school trousers and white shirt and would expect me to clean it ready for the next school day! Children have such simple faith that mum can miraculously make their clothes clean with absolutely no effort! Eventually, we had to agree that, with the days drawing out, David would come home first, get changed, then meet up with his friends to go and play football. That way, I could preserve his school uniform and he could wear his football kit and re-wear it until it was so utterly dirty that it had to be washed. Daniel was desperate to go and play football with his brother but we did not think that was wise, especially if they kicked the ball hard or wanted to practise tackling. They were, after all, nearly three years older than Daniel.

We had to make sure, therefore, that we either took a football on holiday or promised to buy one or I was sure David would make known his disappointment. (As it happened, it didn't stop me forgetting!)

Daniel was beginning to get his teeth into children's books. I think he must be a naturally fast reader because he didn't seem to take very long to read a book. Whilst he couldn't always tell you the entire contents and in-depth analysis of the book, he certainly seemed to appreciate each book's plot and the main characters. We had lots and lots of Enid Blyton books, some of which David was just beginning to read, but we surmised that they were probably suited for children aged seven or eight and upwards. Nevertheless, Daniel was hungry to read and did not want books which were full of pictures. He certainly was a precocious talent.

We opted to take on holiday several of the 'Famous Five' books by Enid Blyton, while Barry packed some thrillers by Michael Crichton and John Grisham for us to read. I think Barry was ready for a good holiday doing as little as possible. It sounded like we would have plenty of opportunity to relax by the swimming pool and read either in the sun or in the shade, whatever our preference was.

Fortunately for us, Tenerife was not in the European Community at the time (I don't think it is now) and Barry had read that it would be very cheap to eat out or buy food and drink whilst we were there. Also, we would be able to get money by using our bank card so we only needed to take a small amount of currency with us and maybe just a couple of hundred pounds in travellers cheques.

It was exciting. We were going on a plane from Gatwick airport. Rather than fiddle about with parking our car, we reasoned that it would be a lot less hassle to hire a taxi. That way, the onus was on the local taxi company and their driver to get to our house promptly on the morning of our departure and deliver us safely to the airport. We planned to arrive well before our departure so that the boys could watch the 'planes arriving and departing. That would be a new experience for them, and they loved it. They spent ages perched on the leather chairs, leaning forward as planes came and went with relentless frequency. The decision to take a taxi proved an excellent one.

The flight itself was very enjoyable. I think David, Daniel and I were all slightly on tenterhooks when the plane made that strange accelerating noise and began to nose upwards ready for take off. It's a strange feeling suddenly being airborne in a heavy metal container with imitation bird wings. Both children grimaced and grabbed my side: I had one each side of me while Barry sat in the opposite set of three seats.

The children were highly amused when the stewardess started delivering the meals to passengers. They thought it was great that we should have dinner on the plane. They weren't so impressed when they saw what the dinner was, and neither of them ate much of it. Fortunately, for just such an occasion, a mother always carries a supply of sweets in her handbag, and that kept them satisfied for the journey.

I suppose we thought we would arrive at the airport, walk out the door and the hotel would be a few yards down the road. Not so. We were directed towards a collection point by the tour operator's representative where a coach would "transfer" us to our hotel. About an hour later, maybe less, we arrived in the resort called Los Gigantes. I can't say it looked that inspiring, although we have subsequently returned to Tenerife and visited it again and it has substantially improved.

By the time we arrived, the children were getting fractious and hungry. Ignoring the state of the resort's "development" – there were lots of patches of dusty land and it was clear that other hotels were in the course of being finished off, what with various builders' and workmen's vans everywhere – the hotel and the room itself looked very nice. It was so hot. Fortunately, the room was air-conditioned. The floor was nice and cool to walk on, made of marble-effect slabs. The shower was wonderful: nice and hot and plenty of power. We even had a television if we wanted to watch it. There were two big bedrooms: one for the boys and one for us. All the beds were single, which from our point of view was probably just as well because it would have been so hot otherwise. This way, we would not have to resort to arguing if one or other of us wanted to discard the covers.

By the time we had put on some lighter clothing and had a quick wash, it must have been nine o'clock. That was okay: we were on holiday. David thought it was great fun staying up late. We took a little wander outside the hotel and headed towards a restaurant within a short distance of a little stretch of beach. There is something special about eating a meal overlooking water, I believe. Barry seemed relaxed, and both boys were behaving very well. We could see that various trips left the resort on a regular basis, either to do a tour around that part of the coast or we could take a trip and swim with the dolphins. That appealed to Barry, but the children were not able to swim at that time. That was something I determined to address on getting back to England. At least that way they would not miss out on the opportunity to swim in the sea with us in the future.

It must have been about ten-thirty, maybe eleven, by the time we walked back into the hotel. It was dusk outside, but the night air had that exotic or tropical feel about it where there is no real urgency to go to bed. Lots of street lights and the hotel lights shone and we could hear a resonating rhythm from crickets, although we couldn't see them anywhere. The karaoke session was just drawing to a close by the swimming pool, and it sounded as if the resident disc jockey had become tired of singing to the equally tired audience. The pool was officially closed from ten to allow for pool cleaning, not that it stopped some of the more playful residents trying their luck at "skinny dipping" in the early hours, so we found out the following morning. Shocking! You can only blame it on the warm air, I suppose.

Both boys were almost asleep on their feet. Tomorrow, we could have an easy day sitting or lounging by the swimming pool and let the boys swim, or more to the point, play in the pool. It wasn't very deep so that was a big relief, and it would help them to keep cool.

We got back to our room and got the children settled down before beginning to settle down ourselves. Barry noticed something strange on one of the wardrobe doors. Just as well he did and attended to it otherwise I might have screamed the place down. Carefully, he approached the door whilst I had my eyes shut. I heard him get out of bed and turned to see what he was doing. I think he was equally nervous about what he was doing. He opened the door to the apartment in readiness for his next move, then returned to where he had been before flicking something onto the floor and kicking it on the floor and out into the passageway. A cockroach had planned to lodge with us for the night! In the morning we mentioned it to the receptionist who assured us that all rooms were fumigated regularly but that on rare occasions, the odd cockroach did make the daring attempt to lodge in the hotel without paying the appropriate tariff! However, I was too tired to worry about whether any of its friends were in the neighbourhood, although Barry said it played on his mind for a while.

After a great sleep, we eventually got up at ten the next morning. We indulged in a breakfast of cereals and fruit juice on the basis that if we ate light we could avoid worrying about jumping in the swimming pool without letting the food properly digest. So, after a quick return to our apartment, we toddled downstairs to head for the pool. Barry had his John Grisham book to hand and I had my Maeve Binchy book, which I hoped would be a light read, along with a bag containing towels and sun cream. It was scorching hot; absolutely lovely. The boys were in their element in the pool, and with Barry engrossed in the twists and turns of his book's plot, it fell to me to jump in the pool and enjoy playing games with David and Daniel who had some simple protective armbands. We splished and splashed but we could have done with a ball. That omission was resolved when a nice young English boy, probably the same age as David, invited the boys to play with him. That enabled me to get back to my book and relax, knowing that children can keep themselves occupied for long times if they are enjoying playing. Later, they had a young German boy who joined them to play, which was nice. We met his parents, along with the English boy's mother. They all seemed pleasant, but I must admit I did struggle to get along with the German couple. They spoke very good English, but were a little tiresome for me unfortunately. Perhaps it was my perception of their Germanic efficiency, or maybe I just found them arrogant.

The good thing was that both boys found themselves playmates and that always takes some of the pressure off you when you are on holiday with children. What a relaxing day we had. Barry takes a long time to unwind because he has such an important job, so it was good that he could engross himself in his book and take his mind off work. That would set him up for the rest of his holiday. If he felt he had achieved something, even if it was reading one book, he could relax enough to give the children his attention and spend time enjoying them.

I won't bore you with accounts of all our comings and goings at meal times, but the highlight has to be when we went into a restaurant whilst we were there and Barry ordered lobster from the menu. The waiter invited him to the tank to select the appropriate creature so the boys followed their daddy to the tank, wondering what was going to happen next. After carefully extracting the unfortunate victim, the boys were keen to know where the lobster would go. You have to be so careful what you say to young children, don't you, or it can cause them all sorts of trauma! Regrettably, Barry perhaps did not appreciate what impact it would have in telling the boys the lobster would be put in a pot of boiling hot water to cook. Daniel looked very puzzled, and David looked horrified. Whilst Daniel did not say anything because he reasoned, I believe, that this was impossible because the creature was still alive, David, being a more sensitive soul, began to weep thinking it would cause the poor creature unbearable suffering. We then had to explain that the lobster did not feel any pain, and Barry felt he had to try and rescue the situation with a little untruth that the lobster had been put to sleep and was already dead before it was cooked. I'm not sure how badly it affected David, but I don't think he has ever eaten lobster. As it happened, Barry said it tasted fantastic and it was the best meal he had whilst we were there. For the boys, we tended to stick to what we thought were safe options, namely chicken or occasionally ordinary fish. Daniel was not particularly keen on the taste or texture of fish but David, rather surprisingly, had quite a liking for it.

Wonderfully hot sunny days came and went, one after another. Barry started to tan very nicely. He was getting through his book. Mine was proving a little bit more of a struggle, probably because I was keeping an eye on the children whilst they were swimming, but I tried to snatch some reading time when we were settling down for the night, or if we opted for a little siesta because it did get incredibly hot around about one-thirty/two o'clock.

Unfortunately, both David and Daniel burned on their first full day so they were a little uncomfortable for a couple of days whilst their skin adjusted to the exposure. We had thought that it would be better to put cream on after they came out of the pool, especially as we reasoned that if everyone smothered their children in cream before going in the pool, the water would be utterly horrid and swimming with oil. But, if the option was to avoid my children getting burned, then the pool would have to be a little more oily.

It was a nice little resort, Los Gigantes, despite it needing some attention to its general appearance. There were lots of restaurants and easy walks; we even found a man-made enclosure, which after high tide left a natural swimming pool. The boys loved that: just beyond the enclosure was the Atlantic Ocean pounding against a concrete boundary from where some of the locals would try a spot of fishing. We saw some massive crabs which really thrilled the boys, but we had to be careful because if they fell over the edge, I am sure the current was quite strong and neither Barry nor I were that strong a swimmer. But, on a few occasions, we took food and drinks and spent hours there letting the boys swim in the natural pool, occasionally squealing with delight because they could see the fish or one of the fish had brushed against their leg. There were several areas where folks could lay out their towels and sun-bathe or sit peacefully, keeping an eye on their children in the pool. We found it a very relaxing place to go. It was less noisy. There were no tensions related to whether you had taken the sun lounge that some other person claimed was theirs. All that stereotyping of Germans doing this by the hotel swimming pool was unfortunately true. But I have to say some of the English people were not particularly good in this respect.

On one of the days, we decided we would go on the boat in search of the dolphins. The captain of the small boat assured all of us on board -about twenty-five of us - that we would definitely see the dolphins. No fish were supplied to throw to them, which I thought was a little disappointing. (I remembered years previously I had gone to Longleat and we had been entranced by the sea-lions racing alongside the river boat and taking the scraps of fish we threw to them.) It was amazing to us to see how clear the sea was: entrancing and slightly unsettling because it was very very deep.

We must have been out at sea less than ten minutes when the captain slowed the boat close to a beautiful alcove. And then we saw them. There must have been eight or ten of them. Beautiful creatures. The captain increased the speed and the dolphins surfed in and out of the water following us for about five minutes. Barry took lots of pictures, which we still have. The boys thought the dolphins were great and, just like a young child does, Daniel expressed a desire to take one home with us. He was extremely upset when we said that was not possible, but eventually grasped that dolphins were huge creatures and need to live in a big sea. Daniel still has a number of ceramic and toy dolphins on display in his bedroom. Clearly, they made a big impression on him. David was similarly inspired by them but he seemed to absorb the wonder of watching the dolphins swim and store the experience away in his psyche.

We were very conscious that the children were young and wanted to play in the water and generally have fun rather than go off sight-seeing. That could wait for another time, although Barry and I desperately wanted to go and see the volcano. As it turned out, we got on very well with the mother of the nice English boy who had invited David and Daniel to play with him. When we were telling her about what an awesome thing it was to be so near a volcano and that it would be good to go and see it perhaps the next time we came, she had no hesitation in offering to keep an eye on the children if we wanted to go and see it.

We were very fortunate to be able to go up El Teide. The crater is huge and stretches for many kilometres, but the further you go up the mountain the harder it is to breathe. We witnessed truly stunning views, and it was awesome to think that the crater had fallen in on itself as opposed to the volcano having erupted. Thankfully, it appears to be a dormant volcano. I'd hate to think of the consequences if it ever started to 'breathe' again!

All around Los Gigantes, there were the most gorgeous flowers. Everyone who owned a villa or a property seemed to have the most beautifully coloured garden with a rich variety of colours and unusual flowers. From the hotels, as you walked up the hills to the shopping areas, you could see – they are probably still there – a network of pipes to help keep the soil irrigated and to avoid any shrubs and flowers perishing in the heat.

Some of the evenings we made use of the hotel bar and took up our chairs to join in the time of karaoke. Barry had a go one night...eventually. I think he had three or four San Miguels before he had the courage to take up the microphone and give his own special rendition of "Allright now". It had been a long time since he had done any public singing and I was surprised how nervous he was. David was very confident and was desperate to do some singing and had a go at doing "American Pie" much to his brother's amusement. I'm not sure why but the d-j had the full version, so after about four minutes of David doing the song the best justice he could, the sound was faded so that someone else could have a chance. It was good fun, and everybody seemed to enjoy themselves.

We had ten days of wonderful holiday out in Tenerife and were very sad when our stay drew to a close. Barry had the most gorgeous tan. Both boys looked the picture of rude health, and I must admit I was quite pleased with my own colour. So it was on the Tuesday morning, having gathered our luggage, we abandoned it in a secure room so that we could have one last wander around the town before the coach collected us at twelve noon. We had taken lots of photos. We had found some interesting little mementos to take back with us as a reminder of the wonderful time we had spent in Los Gigantes along with a few modest gifts for mum, Edna and Shirley. Barry bought a bag of sweets as a little thought for his work colleagues (after some prompting from me). We would miss the giants, the cliffs after which the town was aptly named, and the natural pool and the hotel and the karaoke. Unfortunately, we missed the nice lady who looked after David and Daniel because she left on the Saturday. I feel rather embarrassed that I can't remember her name, but if she should read this one day, at least she will know we appreciated her kindness.

It's a terrible feeling of coming back down to earth when you return from a wonderful holiday, isn't it? You wonder if your life will ever be the same again. We had an easy flight back to England, and reliable as Big Ben, there was our taxi driver when we got through reclaiming our luggage at the airport. We seemed to arrive in Hungerford in no time at all, and, after tipping the driver, we were back in our own home, a little tired after the journey. It felt much cooler, but then again, compared to Tenerife I suppose it would. Even the sky looked unhappy, but we have to press on with life, don't we? The boys had the rest of their summer holidays to look forward to and we needed to find another bigger house.

CHAPTER 28

WE NEED A BIGGER HOUSE IN THE COUNTRY

August flew by. Having enjoyed such a wonderful holiday, lazing in the pool and splashing around, it seemed a good time to cement David and Daniel's love of water and enrol them in swimming lessons, as well as to take them swimming at every available opportunity. Barry took a few more days' holiday leave towards the end of August which enabled us to dash off to Bournemouth for a few days' in a static caravan, which was good fun. Not as good as Tenerife, but adequate given the lovely weather and ease of access to the lovely beaches at Sandbanks and at Branksome Chine. It certainly did us the power of good and set us up for the new school year and planning a house move.

We both thought Dorset was a lovely county and that it would be great to live nearer to the sea, but Reading would be rather a long journey whichever way we looked at it. So, for the time being, Dorset was out. Very disappointing, especially as we had enjoyed a leisurely drive through some of the Dorset villages during our stay in the static caravan. Some of the villages had lovely names, but one village that particularly appealed to us was called Ryme Intrinseca. What a great name! It was very close to a village with another wonderful name, Yetminster, which rather reminded me of a comedy programme which had been broadcast on the television in the 1980's. (No doubt, it still does the rounds on the satellite stations which endlessly repeat all the comedies of the 1970's and '80's, ad tedium.)

We really needed somewhere in Hampshire or Berkshire, preferably close to the M3 or A33 and ideally within an hour's drive of Reading. Bearing in mind we were looking for a nice house in the country, it narrowed down our options. Andover was out of the question because it was just a little too far in our opinion and whilst Basingstoke was very pleasant, we really did not want to live in a town if we could help it. No wonder the so-called 'experts' say that moving house is one of our most stressful experiences.

Meanwhile, during the summer holidays, Daniel enjoyed reading his books. David enjoyed playing lots of football with his friends and sometimes would pick up his toy guitar while he played some of Barry's old 45s on the turntable of our antiquated music system. The football season was just about to get started and David was also keen to get into a football team, and some of his young friends were hoping to join with him. Whether that would become a reality we didn't know; we merely hoped that he could play on Saturdays if there were to be matches.

September was soon upon us and we were none the wiser about where we should move to. (Okay, so I should ideally put 'to which village or location we should move'! Grammar isn't everything!) North Waltham, being close to the M3, was full of rustic charm, with lots of older buildings and a good feel to it, and there certainly seemed to be lots of things we could get involved in, but we were unwilling to commit ourselves yet. Of the other villages nearby, neither of us relished the prospect of being too much further from the motorway, so at least we were getting closer to a decision.

Daniel resumed nursery at See-Saws but Mrs Fellingham was convinced that there was a very real possibility that, because he was making such good progress with his learning, Daniel really should get into mainstream schooling at the earliest opportunity. Realistically, we thought that it would be next September, but Mrs Fellingham encouraged us not to give up hope. He would be four in the January and was rapidly catching up David with his reading ability.

David seemed settled in the primary school, and there was great news within a short time of him starting the new school year: the school had been able to get a local building company to sponsor them with shirts for the football teams. In the previous school year, a new teacher had been taken on and it turned out that he not only loved taking the sports lessons but also was a great enthusiast for young children developing their sporting prowess early. Having settled into a routine, he had apparently expressed an interest in getting football teams running and was willing to liaise with other schools in arranging football fixtures. David and his friends were very excited and even more so when they were selected to play.

Both Daniel and I went along to David's first game. It wasn't like you see on the television. Instead, it seemed to be played very chaotically with the children crowding each other all the time, a bit like that scene in "Bedknobs and Broomsticks" when all the animals have that crazy game of football! I can't remember whether David scored, but I do remember him being covered in grass stains and dirtying his kit. I wondered whether any of the teachers at his next school would have the same enthusiasm for sports, especially football, knowing how disappointed David would be if the answer proved negative.

I guess you could say that I have always been a fan of English literature, going right back to my school days. I am not saying I am extremely well-read, or a master (or mistress for the politically correct brigade!) of the subject, but there is something wonderful about a well-written book. I really don't care for some of the modern creations with their liberal use of blasphemy, awful swearing and crudeness. Not when you can pick up something which has the power to affect you without resorting to such expletives. Not long ago I read Mary Shelley's "Frankenstein" and was moved to pity for that poor creation.

(Anyway, I am in digression mode again. Sorry!)

You can imagine my surprise, I hope, when one day in the autumn of that year, Daniel was kneeling in front of the bookcase, running his fingers over the book covers. He was not yet four years of age. Something took his fancy, probably the picture on the cover, and he decided that was the book we should read. Most days, I read with Daniel for a few minutes, but I couldn't maintain concentration for too long because I was always conscious of either getting tea ready or some other task which merited my attention, or the need to ensure that I did not overlook spending time with David. I must admit, I thought "I hope he hasn't got out one of the Dickens novels. That really is too mature for him to grasp". No, he had not. What he had opted for was that delightful novel – or should I say account? – by Gerald Durrell of his upbringing on the island of Corfu in "My family and other animals".

It's so important that children are encouraged to read and to love books from a young age, in my humble opinion, and to ensure that they are properly guided so that they don't become disillusioned with learning. Well, that's what I think. It certainly hasn't harmed my children. Daniel has read the most astounding breadth of books since, and I credit some of David's ability to write his own lyrics for his band to his early love of reading. Admittedly, he followed the more traditional route of being given various reading assignments by his teachers and reading when he had to rather than wanting to have one book or another on the go at any one time. Strange in some ways, I suppose, because other than when he was on holiday, I think the children would probably only have seen Barry reading the newspaper or some papers from work.

Daniel's selection of this book was such a key landmark in his own educational development that I have included it here.

Before Christmas, we were contacted by an agent acting on behalf of a buyer regarding our property which we had advertised through one of the more up-market agents. I think I have said earlier that we were not desperate to sell our house in Chilton. Our greater concern was to find for ourselves another property in the right location. The contact by the buyers' agents seemed an unusual approach because we had agents acting on our behalf so we couldn't understand why we had been approached directly. It turned out that this was a new venture sponsored by the agents themselves with a view to developing their services for their clients. This new company would approach people whose houses were on the market and negotiate a deal for their client. The benefit to the seller someone else was actively finding a buyer for them. The benefit to the buyer was that someone went and found a property for them and tried to get the price lowered in the process. That was just what we wanted someone to do for us!

As regards the firm who contacted us, they wanted to set up a viewing for one of their representatives with a view to making an offer on behalf of a client. I couldn't understand why they would do that if their client had not actually seen the property. They said their client used to live in the village many years ago and was very familiar with the particular cul-de-sac where our house was situated, and was also aware that we had made many excellent improvements to the house. It sounded quite promising. I won't bore you with the details other than to say that, true to their word, a very well-dressed woman, probably in her early thirties, came to the property one Saturday morning and was very thorough in looking over all the rooms and the garden. She asked some searching questions. On the Tuesday following, a gentleman phoned us to offer £20,000 less than the asking price of the property. Very disappointing.

Having declined their offer as pleasantly as possible, Barry and I agreed that we should find out more what they could do for us. We clarified our desired specification for the property, location being preferably near the M3 or dual carriageway, the right side of Southampton and definitely no more than an hour's journey to Barry's work at BAD. We set an upper price limit and agreed a commission for them to find us a property and a percentage of any sum by which they could get the asking price reduced. It was nearly Christmas so we did not expect anything until the new year. We were not disappointed!

In due course, we were contacted by the company's representative in mid-January to indicate that they had reviewed two properties, one of which sounded moderately promising, the other apparently being under offer. Four bedrooms, a self-contained annex, wonderful location but not particularly big gardens. Also, it was a very prestigious property in the village. The details were subsequently sent to us and, sure enough, it looked the "quintessential cottage" the estate agent's particulars asserted it to be. Maybe I expected the price to be much higher. I was a little disappointed about the garden size, but at least with the annex mum would be able to move there if she still wanted to. Barry was not very keen.

Hindsight is a wonderful thing. Looking back, I'm not sure why we opted to buy the property because we were not in any big rush. Maybe the prospect of not having too big a mortgage, close access to the motorway, beautiful village and an expectation of getting very involved in its local community. Or, probably more to the point, the fact that our agent had negotiated forty-five thousand pounds off the asking price if we could exchange contracts to purchase the property before the end of February! And that's exactly what we achieved. We lived in North Waltham less than a year, which we acknowledge was neither ideal for the boys or for mum. However, it's all part of the experience of living, isn't it?

The house itself was wonderfully refurbished. It had a rich history going back many many years and had one time been a shop in the village. Nearby, we could see the village pond, so at least we had a wonderful view.

I suspect that, in many ways, we had been completely spoiled by living in such a lovely house in Chilton with such great neighbours and friends and a real sense of belonging to the community. Moving was much more of an emotional upheaval than I had anticipated. For me, the chemistry was not there, and I know that sounds very airy-fairy. I missed Edna's forthrightness, although we did have her to stay one weekend, and she and mum had a great time together. I also missed Mrs Fellingham and village characters like Bob and Shirley. David missed being in the football team. The village school at the time did not share his former teacher's enthusiasm for having football teams at such a young age. Daniel was happy enough because Mrs Fellingham had put in a word for him with the head teacher of the local infant school which David would be attending until the end of that July. And, generally, I think Barry, being a fairly placid man, took the view that he had easy access to work so he was perhaps not as unsettled as we were by the move. Nevertheless, our short stay in North Waltham was memorable for a certain landmark event which we must relate.

CHAPTER 29

DANIEL'S FIRST DAY IN SCHOOL (EARLY SIGNS OF GENIUS)

Having exchanged contracts on the Monday before the end of February, we moved into what we would be our new home on March 8th. I know that seems very specific, but don't you keep your old diaries? We decided to hang on to the Chilton property for the time being.

Mum had put her own village house on the market back in September but only one couple had viewed the property so it looked like there would be some delay before she could move in to the annex. As it turned out, what with our reservations about the property soon after moving in, mum opted not to move to Hampshire. Instead, she came and stayed with us regularly, which the children loved.

The property was in an idyllic location and had been very tastefully renovated by a previous owner but we just felt it was not big enough for us. Barry used the annex for his study and found it particularly helpful for those rare occasions when he needed to work from home.

By the March of 1996, Barry was regularly out of the country on behalf of BAD. I lost track of which countries he had been to because he seemed to be abroad two or three times a month. Brazil, Paraguay, Columbia, Mexico, America, Iceland, Switzerland, Norway. You name the country and there was a chance he had been there to try and win more business for the company whilst still looking after UK 'operations'. Certainly the company seemed very happy with him. He had a wonderful bonus the preceding Christmas, anticipating which we had ordered a Christmas hamper from Harrods. Wonderful! A bit of a luxury, I know, but we wanted to treat ourselves.

David started immediately at infant school and I would not deny that it was a very unsettling experience. The children from the village were a little more demure, shall we say, and were not ready for much 'rough and tumble', although he managed to get on with two boys who were as enthusiastic about football as he was. Daniel stayed at home with me for a few weeks and we did various craft activities and lots of reading.

Mrs Gruba was the headmistress of the infant school and we both met with her on March 18th (I checked my diary). Daniel was perfectly behaved and responded well to the few questions she asked him. She had studied Mrs Fellingham's letter (they were both in the same teachers' union apparently and had served together on some committee). Following our meeting, Mrs Gruba confirmed that she would be happy to let Daniel join the school early. He could start on the Tuesday following the Easter holiday, April 16th, because this would let the other children settle in and that would enable Daniel to be welcomed perhaps more readily than if all the other children were adjusting to being back in a school environment.

The day started off with a crisp breeze and lots of blue sky and developed into one of those gorgeous sunny April days which inspire confidence of lots of further forthcoming hot weather. Daniel looked a proper little schoolboy with his charcoal grey shorts and navy jumper. I was very proud of him and was confident he would do well. All three of us walked to school together that April morning, David humming away some tune or other and Daniel the picture of concentration. After exchanging kisses, I left them together in the playground with all the other children and walked home, turning frequently to see if they were still there, anticipating the bell ringing to call them into the building for registration.

I don't want to generalise but I can't say that I had been made to feel welcome when I had seen any of the other mothers when dropping David off at the school in the first few weeks we were in the village. Different people come and go, don't they, so I don't want you to get the wrong idea of people who might live there today. I think we did get one 'welcome' card from one of the neighbours, but sometimes you instinctively know when you are probably in the wrong place, don't you?

Daniel's first day came and went with no difficulties. Sometimes you worry about whether your child will have an embarrassing accident because of excitement, worry or nerves or whether they will retreat into a shell. Daniel's first few days, according to Mrs Gruba, were very promising. She had been impressed with the feedback she had received from the teachers and from what she had seen of him when she had popped into some of his classes. What she had not anticipated is how genuinely far forward Daniel was with his reading. When books were given out for reading assignments, Daniel would gobble up the book allocated to him there and then because they were so elementary and then hand it straight back to the teacher. The idea was that the book would be taken home with a little notebook so that the parent could confirm the date of reading and add their own comments, so Daniel's precocious reading skill did not fit into the school's system very well. This posed a dilemma because a teacher does not want to quench a child's enthusiasm for learning or to suggest that the child is telling fibs. I remember something similar happening to me, only I would have been about six, I think. I had read a whole book after school but because I could not remember the entire plot and discuss it that well, the teacher did not accept that I had read it so I could not progress to the next book ('Wide range readers', they were called.)

Mrs Gruba met me in the playground one morning when I was dropping off Daniel and David, seeking some insight on Daniel's reading ability. I explained that he was a very precocious little boy and had always been fascinated with reading and had an unusual ability to concentrate for one so young. When I shared about him reading the Gerald Durrell book, her brow positively furrowed so much you could have rolled marbles down the channels! She was grateful because it meant that she could alert the teachers accordingly. Also, it might mean that, with some careful planning and sensitivity, Daniel could receive a little one-to-one tuition and perhaps be recommended by Mrs Gruba to the headmaster for early admission to the local junior school. This happened only in very rare instances, but Mrs Gruba thought that Daniel was so intellectually forward for his years, the only concern was whether he would fit in with mainstream education. Had we thought about arranging private tuition and perhaps entering him for examinations with the consent of the local education authority? Wow! This sounded very exciting. I agreed to discuss it with Barry, not sure that I wanted Daniel to come out of mainstream education. My immediate concern was that he would be disadvantaged if he missed out on the social aspect of education, namely interacting with other pupils and understanding the need to get along with others.

After discussing the matter with Barry, we felt that if we could get the best of both opportunities it would be a good result. Speaking with Mrs Gruba, she agreed to contact the local head and see whether he would admit Daniel in the September of '97 and that would give the infant school time to prepare Daniel over the next academic year. As regards examinations, if Daniel continued with his broad range of reading, there was a real possibility he could sit the GCSE English Literature examination by 2001. He would only be nine! It seemed we had our very own child prodigy. To achieve that target, however, would depend on whether Daniel would be able to use his reading skills as a platform from which to recall content and show good reasoning and good written communication ability. Daniel may not have felt nervous by all this looking ahead at his academic ability. I certainly did. Even now, it makes feel a little tired just meditating on how far Daniel has progressed in his relatively short life.

For the remainder of the term, Mrs Gruba's plan was to introduce Daniel to addition, multiplication and division to get him started on basic mathematics. Daniel was the ideal student. With his predisposition to concentrate, by the end of the academic year, when he was still only four and a half, he had made good progress with elementary sums involving addition or deduction and he could recount his two and three times tables. Over the summer that changed as he drove his older brother to distraction, constantly repeating numbers and asking for David's help. David himself was still in the learning process and did not have the same tendency to academia as his younger brother, so that in some respects Daniel had already overtaken David with his ability in mathematics. The fighting continued, and I won't say any more on that…yet.

Barry wisely kept a low profile during this upheaval. In a strange way, Daniel's development was quite an astounding metamorphosis. While the norm for children of his age would be to please their parents because potty training has been mastered, or because they have gone through the night without wetting the bed, or better still without disturbing their parents' sleep, with Daniel that was a distant memory. We were thinking of getting him to do violin lessons to try and balance his insatiable desire for academic learning but procrastinated on that for the time being. Truly, we had a genius within the family. How blessed we were, we are.

CHAPTER 30

ENJOYING FAMILY LIFE

When Daniel had joined the infant school, it felt like a big step forward for us as a family. I am sure it is not the same as when your children reach an age when they leave home but nevertheless it is a milestone, isn't it? In the September, when Daniel settled into an academic year where the objective was to get him ready for junior school in the year following, it felt like the pieces were falling into place. Barry was due to fly to Uganda at the end of September for some sort of conference. I don't know, but I come from a generation where Uganda is associated with the name Idi Amin, who seemed to be a terrible tyrant (a little bit of alliteration there for those who like that sort of thing). I didn't realise just how many people's deaths he was responsible for, or that he was a known admirer of Hitler, or that he only died in 2003. Barry is a fount of all knowledge, although he tells me a lot of the information can be found on the internet quite easily. I certainly was not overly comfortable with the prospect of my husband being in such a country even though Amin was no longer the president. The fact that Barry was very nonchalant about the visit probably helped me to be a little more assured and less fretful than I would otherwise have been, even though he informed me on his return that it was not his best experience.

As regards the junior school, it had a football team for the seven to nine year olds which David and his two friends found hard to break into. That was a big disappointment for him, although he did get to be a substitute for some of the games during the academic year, but it left him feeling very deflated and hungry to join a local team. Sadly, even that proved fruitless. Fortunately, boys are usually imaginative, so with his friends and some other lads they managed to rope in, they often went down the rec', or Cuckoo Meadow as it had been called in the past. The rec' had been endowed to the village by one William Rathbone, a local landowner, back in the 1950's, which I thought showed great generosity of spirit. The boys, with their footballs in hand, or bouncing them on the path, would go there and play for a while when the evenings were lighter, as well as at the weekends. Daniel was not a keen footballer, which was fortunate for the older boys who would usually come back to our house for a drink of fruit juice and biscuits after enjoying together each of their exciting exploits and high-scoring games.

There must be something about February. Maybe it is the imminence of spring, snowdrops usually being visible and the first signs of daffodils coming through and some of the trees evidencing buds. Whatever it is, both Barry and I felt we wanted to move out of the village. We didn't discuss it with the boys. Fortunately, the property market was now in a much better state. Prices were edging forward very slowly, so we anticipated getting a reasonable price for the North Waltham property. Meanwhile, we had employed an estate agency to look after the letting of the Chilton property and regular income was coming in from them. We decided we would look again at Ryme Intrinseca. It was a long way from Reading, but given the fact that Barry was out of the country on a regular basis, our concern that he should not have far to travel was not a good enough excuse to avoid moving there. We abandoned the idea of using a buying agent, Barry opting to search on the internet on a regular basis and to resort to the traditional method of asking for the estate agents local to Intrinseca to send us details. We took some long leisurely journeys in the car to look around the village and view various properties by appointment over a few weekends in March before eventually finding our dream property.

We won't tell you exactly where it is because we don't want thousands of visitors suddenly descending on us out of curiosity, but we can say that we found a seven-bedroom property with wonderful gardens and great countryside views and with a separate, self-contained annex for mum. It was very expensive and we had to ask the bank for a huge mortgage, but with Barry's salary and our investments, the bank were more than happy to give us the loan we wanted.

Barry had turned forty in the February of '97 and I turned forty in the March, only a few days after our offer on the Intrinseca property had been accepted, so it was a cause for double celebration. Barry was out of the country at the time of his own special birthday, which was very disappointing for us all, but we made sure mum came to stay with us for a week which would include my fortieth birthday. At least that meant we could go out and celebrate with a meal together. Shirley, the sweet thing, had remembered from former conversations that this year would be my fortieth and sent me a lovely card with a big 40 on it.

David, probably influenced by a few of the older lads with whom he played football, was at this time showing more of an interest in popular music, and had taken a liking, I recall, to one particular rock group called Oasis. I suspect they reminded him a bit of some of his dad's old records that he still liked to play from time to time. Whatever was the truth, we had to buy him their album, which he played over and over.

Before the year was out, to encourage David in his singing generally, we decided to invest in an acoustic guitar - not the full size - so that he could do with it whatever he wanted, and if that meant making up songs or getting lessons, we would happily invest in them. David was showing signs of becoming more and more discontented with being contained in an educational environment to the extent that we received a couple of letters complaining about his behaviour. Apparently, he had a stubborn streak and would not always comply with requests to deal with tasks set by his teachers. Our firstborn was a little strong-minded. I didn't mind that, but I didn't want it to be used by others against him to his disadvantage.

Daniel continued to make excellent progress with his reading and with his maths that academic year. We broke the news to Mrs Gruba that we would not, unfortunately, be able to take advantage of all her hard work in liaising with the head of the junior school because we would be moving to Dorset at the end of the school year. Despite this disappointment, Mrs Gruba considered Daniel to be such an exceptional prospect that she committed to contacting the headmaster of a primary school near to Intrinseca about admitting Daniel, and even if he declined, she would happily recommend him to any other school we considered sending him to. What a nice lady to do that! I made sure Barry ordered a big bouquet of flowers for her for the last day of the school term before the summer holidays.

Early August ('97, if you're trying to keep up with where we are in terms of the year) we were able to move into Intrinseca. Immediately, we sensed we were exactly where we supposed to be. There was a WI that I found straight away, or rather I should confess a friendly neighbour told me about it. Thelma was not in the same league as Edna, but was a very nice person. Sadly, she died very recently. Also, there was a Conservative Club close to hand, and I was keen to get my teeth into that as soon as possible. Probably all that 'life begins at forty' thing.

There was a great little recreation ground nearby, and straightaway David and Daniel made friends with children of their own age. Everyone seemed so friendly. The day we moved in we must have had eight 'Welcome' cards, including an invitation to a bar-b-q at a very grand house about a minute's walk from our own property. Absolutely everything fell into place, as if it was just what God had planned for us. Mum was able to sell her house. It was quite a wrench for her and she endured quite an emotional send-off from many of the villagers, not to mention the housekeeper and the gardener. By the September, she had moved into the annex, so that gave us all peace of mind, not having to worry about the distance between us.

I think with the repetitiveness of flying on so many business trips, Barry grew tired of it and so we opted for an inland holiday that summer. Tenby, in Wales, looked very inviting, with wonderful beaches where the children could go exploring (under our watchful eyes) and swimming without us having to worry about their safety. As it turned out, we had a fantastic time staying in Tudor Square. We saw the plaque dedicated to Beatrix Potter, who had apparently drawn one of her illustrations for "The tale of Peter Rabbit" whilst staying at a particular residence in 1900. The hotel was good; the views were wonderful. It wasn't quite "It was so good, I bought it", but you get the general idea that we liked what we experienced. So much so, that in the spring of 1998 we bought a lovely six-bedroom cottage about a mile from the town centre, and fortunately we bought before all the property prices were dramatically hiked up. We were able to use the cottage for two holidays the following year, the rest of the time leaving it with a local managing agent to rent it out to carefully screened applicants so that it generated some good income for us.

In the September, thanks to Mrs Gruba's altruistic endeavours, the primary school headmaster admitted Daniel. Mr Fitzwallinghurst was a very stern headteacher and I can't say I really warmed to him, perhaps because he had such a high standard to attain to when compared to Mrs Fellingham and Mrs Gruba. He was a gentleman in his late fifties, very thin hair with something of a comb-over but not a patch (excuse the pun) on the comb-over we encountered when we first met the plumber in Chilton. He retired two years later and I suspect that his enthusiasm for teaching and looking after a school was on the wane.

I believe Daniel might have progressed even quicker if Mr Fitzwallinghurst had taken more of an interest in the child prodigy which he had the good fortune to have under his care. I don't think he discussed Daniel's needs with the teachers because it fell to me to motivate Daniel with his reading and with his maths. All in all, the academic year 1997-8 was something of a come-down after such astonishing earlier developments by Daniel. I had a copy of Tolstoy's "War and Peace" lurking somewhere in the bookshelf and I sincerely hoped that Daniel did not fancy his chances at reading it, let alone Dostoevsky's "Crime and Punishment". With keeping home and attending to the myriad of chores necessary to properly look after the Squits family, I couldn't possibly keep track of which book or books young Daniel would extract and squirrel away in his bedroom. I certainly didn't want him reading some of Barry's thrillers: they might give him nightmares, and from my brief forays into the text of some of them, I didn't want Daniel reading inappropriate language.

David worked as hard as was expected of him by his teachers and his behaviour was less of a problem. The school had football teams and David was in his element as long as he could do sport and had the prospect of maybe singing or having some attention. He even began to like cricket. I think that, in fairness, should be properly accredited to Mr Fitzwallinghurst, who was an ardent fan of Hampshire Cricket Club and was keen to see more cricket played in schools. David loved to leap about, trying to pull off spectacular and impossible catches, like the ones he would probably have seen on the television. He certainly watched a lot of sport, and that worried me to a degree because I thought it would affect his own creativity. Even at such an early age, I believe David was hankering to be famous for being great at something. Every Thursday afternoon, there was music, and the children had the opportunity to learn recorder, guitar or violin. David already had his own guitar so he was happy to learn a bit more how to best play it. I am still not sure to what extent it helped because, in the main, he has taught himself what he wants to play or the music he wants to create. Fascinating how children learn. What happens to suffocate our creativity as we get a little older?

Shirley from Chilton was kind enough to keep in contact with me, so it was nice to get her occasional letters, even though we had moved even further away. In 1998, her oldest child, Nathan, had left home and joined the army. Lucy, her youngest, was about the same age as David, and was making acceptable progress in school. Without disclosing the delicate details, Shirley had experienced a distressing divorce which came through in the January, I believe. And she had just recovered from breast cancer! Some folks do go through the mill with trials, don't they? The people who had subsequently bought our old house in Chilton when we had decided to discontinue renting it out were not particularly pleasant characters and had managed to deeply upset Edna and a few of the other villagers. We always tried to be pleasant neighbours, and when I quizzed Edna about it, she was too upset to dwell on it, so I don't know what that little spat was about.

When school resumed in September, I made a point of expressing my concerns to Mr Fitzwallinghurst about Daniel's progress and he promised to consider ways of exploiting his potential and enlisting the co-operation of his teaching colleagues. Taking a leaf out of Mrs Fellingham's approach, I challenged him to set one or more objectives for Daniel to achieve in the academic year, maybe something like improving his written work and his use of English to communicate good reasoning skills? He submitted only to the point of agreeing to keep it in mind. As I hinted, I think his enthusiasm was on the wane.

A very modest Christmas production was put on by the school. It would be hard to match See-Saws' Christmas performance. It didn't come anywhere near it! David got cast as one of the angels for reasons known only to the teacher in charge of the dramatic production! However, having missed out on being involved in Chilton primary school's abridged version of "Joseph", the local primary school was going to do the full version and planned to put on two performances before the Easter break. David was cast as Joseph! That was such an encouragement for him, to think that he could be chosen for a main part and not feel like a substitute sitting on the sidelines, there just in case the team was desperate.

Christmas 1998 was lovely because we spent it with mum being around the whole time. It was so good to feel a part of the local community. I had attended a few WI meetings, as well as some stimulating discussions hosted by the local Conservative Club. Barry had occasionally joined me at the club, but had usually got distracted at the bar, so he was not involved in any of the actual meetings as such. Mum enjoyed the occasional WI meeting, but was happy to keep herself busy in the adjacent annex and was on hand to help out with baby-sitting for those rare occasions when Barry was able to take himself away from his work and go out for a drink or for a meal.

The boys loved being in the village. I occasionally got along to the Sunday service at the local church but the incumbent did not have the same vibrant personality as Andrew Jones, and I didn't care too much for some of the wishy-washy sermons he gave. Frederick Simolus was his name, I recall. He has since been replaced, but we won't discuss that for the time being.

The distance to Reading didn't pose a great problem for Barry. If he was particularly tired, or anticipated long meetings and tight deadlines, he booked into a nearby hotel at the company's expense. At least that way I could be sure he was safe.

With the new term recommencing in January, work began on the school's production of "Joseph". David was given the songs and the script, and his task was to learn everything off by heart.

And I'll tell you how it went next.

CHAPTER 31

DAVE GETS LEAD ROLE OF JOSEPH

Mum was great to have around because she has the patience of a saint. She was happy to give some of her energy to reading or playing word games with Daniel, or to encouraging David when he was in a creative mood, either to assist with a one thousand piece intricate jigsaw or to give him a gem of helpful advice regarding his breathing for when he had to hold a note. So, when David got the part of Joseph and came home with the script and songs, mum was the ideal person to lend me a hand as David set about the task of learning the production off-by-heart.

Daniel took great delight, as any younger brother would, in taunting David as he practised singing the songs, no doubt in a bid to get some of the attention that was going David's way. In fairness to David, he restrained himself from entering into another fray and the usual associated screaming, shouting and thumping...thankfully. That was probably when we introduced Daniel to Solitaire and found an old Rubik's cube in a bid to keep him distracted and away from David during this important time. In a strange way, this worked out very positively and helped Daniel to develop what might be generally called strategy skills. The biggest challenge it created was getting him to surrender the cube when it was time for him to settle down for the night, and to ensure that he did not let his love of reading slip because of his fascination with solving the puzzle of the cube.

During this time, when mum was supporting David, she reached the milestone of her eightieth birthday. The children thought she was great and had helped me select various gifts from Barry (who was fond of mum), me and from each one of them. We had a lovely shop in nearby Yetminster which sold all sorts of wonderful things and was great to browse in. That, combined with a visit to Yeovil, resulted in mum and all of us enjoying her birthday. We bought the most wonderful broach with a lovely encrusted red ruby which she adored. Notwithstanding the essential bouquet of lilies, together with a separate bouquet of freesias, which were her favourite flowers. We thought it would be rude not to celebrate with a cake and a little party. And that's exactly what we did. We had already invited Edna, who stayed with us for the night, and mum had invited a couple of the ladies with whom she had developed friendships in the village, Daphne and Manilla, both very well-to-do but pleasant with it.

When it came to singing 'happy birthday to you', we encouraged David to get his guitar, and he impressed everyone with the jolly strumming to accompany the singing of the annual greeting. And to finish off the evening, we managed to polish off a couple of bottles of Chateauneuf (not the children, although David did have a little drop from mum's glass), so everyone ended the night very happy and relaxed, ready to handle whatever the next day would bring.

Looking back, the school's decision to attempt a production of something as comprehensive as "Joseph" may have been 'a bridge too far', as they say. The investment of time, not only by the children but also by the parents, must have been collectively a staggering number of hours, and I am not sure that the return on the investment was satisfactory. During the music lesson in school, the children were able to practise the songs, but there were also two after-school gatherings each week. Heading into March, each Saturday morning involved a walk to the school, script in one hand, costume in another. Easter was right at the start of April that year and the school term would end the day after my birthday. All the children were getting more and more fractious as we entered the middle of March, knowing that the following week they would be performing on the Monday, Tuesday and Wednesday nights before finishing school term on the Thursday.

Compared to See-Saws, I have to say the school was a little backward in ensuring that the production got as much publicity as it could have received. It was mentioned after the event in a regional parish magazine and in the local press, but nobody from the local radio station or the local paper came to any of the performances and neither did the mayor or mayoress of Yeovil or Sherborne, the nearest towns. I think there was an advertisement in the local paper and posters around the villages of Yetminster and Intrinseca itself, as well as reminders to parents. Tickets were charged at a modest three pounds per head for adults, and children were free unless their supervising adult wanted to voluntarily contribute an amount. One of the school's front walls was badly in need of either a complete repointing or demolition and rebuilding, so the funds raised would go towards that worthwhile cause.

March 22nd arrived. I wondered whether David was nervous or

would have stage fright, particularly as he had the lead part. Mum was confident that David knew all the lines to the songs and that all would be well. All told, the performance was expected to last about an hour and a half, starting at six o'clock. After school, David was understandably preoccupied with himself and played on his guitar for a while. He was not hungry, which I took to be a good sign. We went back to the school for quarter past five to make sure everyone was in costume and ready for going on stage punctually. Mrs Lyon, the music teacher, would be playing piano to accompany the songs. Two of the parents were in a band and they kindly agreed to support the pianist with drums and bass guitar, so that the overall musical sound was quite professional. Barry was in Switzerland the entire week so he missed his firstborn's nascent singing career which was a real pity and led to us exchanging some strong words.

The main hall was quite well filled for the first night. There were some gaps in the rows of chairs, but thankfully not sufficiently obvious to have caused upset either to the cast or to those parents who had invested their time in the preceding two months. Six o'clock arrived and everyone was ready. After a brief welcome and introduction by the headmaster, we were ready to begin the show. A young narrator did very well between the songs and had obviously been given lots of encouragement to inflect his voice so that he avoided monotone. The musicians seemed relaxed for each of the songs and that was a big relief, because if they were worried it would be bound to affect the children.

The plot was set as Jacob was dwelling in the land of Canaan. You don't need me to tell you the story, do you? David's first song was coming up, and I was naturally anxious for him, whereas Daniel and mum were just revelling in the atmosphere of theatre. And then we were on with the dream song. No problem. He sang it beautifully. My David is a good singer and he had just performed his first song in public! He executed the rest of the songs confidently, mum once or twice glancing at me with nods of assuring approval. The plot worked its way slowly towards the finale where Jacob is reunited with his lost son, Joseph, and the dream song is repeated and blends into 'Give me my coloured coat'. I don't know what David expected, maybe just the usual polite applause, but the audience which had gathered for the first showing cheered and whistled enthusiastically and stood to applaud the entire cast. The headmaster then thanked those who had attended and directed the audience's attention to the very competent contribution made by the musicians who were likewise generously applauded.

We knew we were among friendly people when we first arrived in the village, but that affirmation for my firstborn served only to reinforce the sense that we had arrived in the place where we should be and it would take something momentous to get me to move house again. I think I slowly began to understand why mum and daddy had been so happy to live where they were for all those years, but even mum, who had just turned eighty, seemed to be settling into village life and was the picture of good health. The subsequent performances on the Tuesday and Wednesday nights were similarly well received. Mum faithfully supported her oldest grandson by being present for both performances.

Daniel took the option of staying home with me on the Wednesday night because I had felt very bloated and uncomfortable, which was not the first occasion for me to have experienced such symptoms in recent months. I had seen the doctor and queried whether I was struggling with irritable bowel syndrome, but he assured me that was not the case, although he did encourage me to ensure I avoided fatty foods and eat more vegetables and pulses.

I had never been a fan of hot spicy food, but if I was supposed to eat more beans and lentils, now was the time to start cooking more chilli con carnes. I made sure not to use too much chilli powder in case it upset the boys, and they loved it when I served up a nice big plate of rice and chilli with kidney beans. Maybe it's the texture of rice and kidney beans and the sauce that makes it such an enjoyable meal, but even today Daniel loves it when I cook a chilli. I usually add some brown sugar, which I suspect appeals to his sweet tooth. That was all well and good but by the time we headed into April I had put on two dress sizes and was feeling a little overweight and some occasional backache, although not as bloated as I had been.

David thoroughly enjoyed his singing part in "Joseph". Very thoughtfully, the music teacher and the head arranged for every member of the cast to receive a lovely certificate reminding them of their part in the production and thanking them for their contribution in raising nearly eleven hundred pounds for the school over the three performances.

CHAPTER 32

DANIEL'S PRODIGIOUS PROGRESS

Previously, I mentioned that we introduced Daniel to solitaire and the Rubik's cube to stop him distracting David whilst he was practising for the school's production of "Joseph", and also to encourage him away from seeking to get mum's attention or mine when we were helping David. I am still not sure whether this was the trigger point, or catalyst, for Daniel's next surge in personal development, but during April, Daniel resumed his passion for reading with a vengeance.

Yeovil library was more easily accessible to us than Sherborne, so we made regular trips on the bus, often with mum, not just to browse in some of the quaint shops surrounding St John's church and buy a variety of wonderful cheeses from a lovely delicatessen, but also to spend time in the library. Looking back, I can recall the number of times we left the library with an old carrier bag full of books, most of which were to satisfy Daniel's appetite to learn and acquire knowledge. By the end of April, Daniel was only three squares off solving the Rubik's cube. On umpteen occasions, he had shown me the solitaire set with just two marbles left, much to his annoyance. We had a marble set and a wooden rounded peg set for solitaire, but I rarely got below having three pegs left. It's such a good game for getting you distracted.

Families don't seem to play so many games these days, do they? Everything seems to revolve around the evil eye, that great big monitor in the corner of the living room, and more often than not, in most children's bedrooms. I would not be surprised if many children have poor sight from staring at monitors for such long periods of time. (Get that observation off my chest while I think about it.) Monopoly, that's a good game, but if you are competitive, the sparks can fly when someone buys the property you want, or you keep landing on their square and paying fines to them. Rrrr. Scrabble, now that is excellent for stretching your mind to make words from letters, but how many children do you and I come across who play word games? Bearing in mind, it's one of our key means of communicating, whether we are typing a letter, or filling out an application for a job, or trying to promote a product, surely it's worth spending time with our children playing such word games?

(Sorry, digressing again.)

Daniel…not only brilliant at reading, but beginning to solve puzzles, and only just turned seven years of age. In addition to the books Daniel borrowed from the library, we had lots of books in our house. It's always useful to have some encyclopaedias in the house, not that we ever parted with money for the Encyclopaedia Britannica, but we certainly had a number of single volume encyclopaedias in addition to a twenty-four volume set daddy had given to me when I was eleven. They had a great musty smell that makes you think of what the people must have been like in 'the olden days' before television, or before the war. Maybe an association with 'oldness' and mystique. It makes me want to just handle the book tenderly before thinking about opening it to look at wonderfully simple line drawings, perhaps of a rudimentary sailing boat built by people living in the jungle somewhere, or perhaps some old instrument which used to be a tool in nineteenth century farming.

There is so much knowledge that we can learn. I know that these days the children try and find everything by looking it up on the internet, but even with faster internet connections, sometimes it is so quick to find an encyclopaedia and get the answer from it within minutes without having to go through the rigmarole of going to the computer. Daniel's bedroom was not kept tidy at the best of times, but it's often true of geniuses that they work amidst what appears to be chaos. In addition to having various library books by his bedside, and books and old drinks on his bedside cupboard, I noticed in his bedroom a very old Pears encyclopaedia and a slightly newer Hutchisons Encyclopaedia that we had gained some years previously when joining a book club. Not only was Daniel showing continuing leaps in his grasp of mathematical concepts (not my strongest subject, but Barry was good at it) and reading ability, he was beginning to grasp more general knowledge which I was sure would contribute to his overall education. His teachers noticed it at school and were worried how they would maintain his interest for one or two years, let alone until the usual age at which a child is admitted to senior school.

Mr Fitzwallinghurst had announced that this would be his last year at the school as he would be retiring at the end of term in July. Towards the end of April, we had a meeting to review how best to care for Daniel within the traditional education system when it was so obvious that he had such prodigious talent when it came to learning. For Mr Fitzwallinghurst to verbally acknowledge Daniel's ability meant a lot to me, in a sense vindicating me for my confidence in him and my attempts to bring him up to be a nice well-mannered young boy even with his precocious talent.

There were inadequate financial resources available to the school to provide Daniel with one-to-one tuition, I was informed. Realistically, Daniel could be ready to take all his GCSEs within five or six years, if not before. In the meantime, we needed to protect Daniel to some degree or he would face the cruellest of bullying, not just from his peers but also from older children. It was unlikely that Daniel would be accepted by the head of the nearest senior school until he was at least ten, yet that would be a step backwards for Daniel. Mr Fitzwallinghurst would not be in a position to dictate Daniel's progress and how Daniel's talent would be nurtured from September, although he promised to ensure a comprehensive record was provided for the new headmistress, together with a suggested teaching plan that might assist both Daniel's teachers, his fellow pupils and Daniel during the forthcoming academic year. Looking further ahead, if Daniel were to take his GCSEs at a very young age, what would be done about further education? After all, he could be ready to progress to taking 'A' levels before he had survived the onslaught of puberty!

The end result of our discussion was that we would need to deflect some of Daniel's mental agility away from subjects that he was already grasping to those which he would have to study when following the senior school curriculum. He needed something particularly difficult. That is when we opted to widen Daniel's education. During the next six months, we would enrol him in violin lessons with a view to him taking violin exams each year. Also, we would get him started on learning French, and maybe Spanish if he made too much progress with French, which I always thought was a slightly easier language to learn than Spanish.

Parenting can be such a challenge! You want to do the best for your children and bring them up to be thoughtful and caring members of society, but some of the stress you endure in thinking about what is best for them, and guiding them, can be overwhelming. It doesn't help when your own mum says that you don't stop worrying about your children just because they've left home!

Mum, however, was very supportive at this time. I felt trapped in one respect: I couldn't stop Daniel being so amazingly clever, or try and quench his ability by discouraging him from reading or learning. Whilst he continued to go swimming occasionally with his brother, he had little or no interest in football yet. How thankful I am that now – probably thanks to his older brother's enthusiasm for the game and his constant jabberings about how great Chelsea are – Daniel at least takes more interest in sport, or I think I would have ended up in the psychiatric ward.

Having addressed this mini crisis – or challenge, to sound more positive – I was about to face a new, slightly surprising challenge, and one which would very much change our lives.

CHAPTER 33

SILLY ME, I'M NOT OVERWEIGHT. WELCOME TO LOOS!

With our part in Daniel's fast-track education now under some semblance of control, and with David having delivered his first set of live singing performances, we thought we would be settling back into some degree of normality. I could not have been more wrong! I don't think I'm particularly low on self-esteem and I don't think I am Mrs Wonderful either, but how I managed to miss the blindingly obvious, I don't know.

By the beginning of May, I seemed to have gone up yet another dress size and felt I was getting a bit bigger all round. Occasionally, I suffered with mild backache and I was getting a little distracted because my monthly cycle seemed to have become very erratic, if it was functioning at all. I was reluctant to visit the medical centre, but mum suggested I do so even if it was just to get peace of mind. I reasoned that I had been consuming much more fizzy drinks over the last few months, not to mention the odd glass of Chateauneuf for various celebrations.

An appointment was made for Friday May 7th with a locum doctor with the most wonderful and highly inappropriate surname: Careless! It was strange: I felt guilty for being so overweight, not that I have ever had the biggest appetite or been a particularly big drinker of soft drinks or alcohol. My preference was the stereotypical cup of tea, or occasionally a cup of instant coffee. No doubt the doctor would steer me into reducing the amount of beverages I consumed and recommend that I drink more water and eat fewer biscuits, especially of the chocolate variety. Doctor Careless, who happened to be a very caring and lovely lady despite her surname, checked my blood pressure and probed me with some very personal questions before attending to a delicate physical examination. Some twenty minutes later, when I felt I had returned to a more dignified state of dress, she lowered her stethoscope and swung her chair towards me, looking at me directly with the natural degree of gravitas that most doctors seem to possess or have ingrained into them. "Mrs Squit, my professional opinion is that you are probably eight months pregnant." I remember her saying that very clearly as if she was in front of me now. Shocked? Usually, I would associate something negative with the word 'shocked'. I should have been.

After a lengthy pause, I remember laughing out loud. When I think of the number of women who find pregnancy such a hassle and don't enjoy the experience, sometimes desperate to be induced early so that they can get the delivery of the baby over and done with, here was I on the cusp of being a mother again and not knowing it. I couldn't help but see the funny side of it. I must have been so busy with things in the house and with mum moving in, and with Daniel and David's various exploits, that I completely lost track of my body's normal monthly routine. My initial laughter continued and began to well up with the joyful prospect of another baby being added to the Squit household. "It's bound to be a girl then, "I told the doctor. When she asked why, I said that the weight was all around me and not all out in front. Doctor Careless did not hold with such presumptions.

Hastily, an appointment was made for me to visit Yeovil Hospital to have an ultrasound scan on the following Thursday (thirteenth) to get a more accurate gauge of when the baby was due. Meanwhile, the doctor would make arrangements with the medical centre's health visitor to come to the house in early June, by which time she expected the baby to have been born.

There was no time to lose. As soon as I got home, I was bubbling over with excitement as I shared the news with mum. Understandably, she looked me in rather bemused fashion as if to query whether I had any degree of intelligence not to have realised that my body was telling me something, and probably had been doing so, for the best part of at least six months. I experienced no morning sickness and no real cravings. I then remembered I had hankered after mint ice cream and chocolate orange wafers for a few weeks back in January but had credited that to concentrating on helping David with the "Joseph" script.

Barry was in Switzerland, but I managed to speak with him on his mobile phone. He was stunned, then delighted, then incoherent as he tried to fathom how he could possibly be a father again at the age of forty-two. He was close to concluding some business with NAF Systems, a company BAD had tracked for some years, I suspect with a view to acquiring them. He would be back on the Wednesday and promised to make arrangements so that he could accompany me to the scan, which I thought was very considerate of him. He is such a sweety sometimes. We agreed that meantime we would not discuss the matter with the children until after the scan.

The good news in all of this was, therefore, that I was not overweight because of pursuing an unhealthy diet. Rather, it was a natural accumulation of extra pounds because I was carrying another precious life inside of me, and no doubt I was eating for two, as they say. I was even bigger by the time the following Thursday came around.

Barry and I waited patiently to be seen for our appointment. No doubt, two hundred people had all been given the same appointment time just in case one hundred and ninety-nine didn't turn up on the day! Some forty-five minutes late, we were shown into the room where the equipment was all set up. I won't bore you with the details (you can't make me, ha ha), but Barry and I nearly fell off our chairs when the pleasant Asian nurse told us in her very quiet voice that I would probably have the baby next Thursday! Barry came over all white as if he really had experienced a shock this time. We had no bedroom prepared for the new child. It had been years since we put away the babygrows and children's clothes and carry-cots etcetera. That was probably the start of Barry's hair changing colour!

Perhaps needless to say, mum was quite nonchalant about the news. Maybe she reasoned that if I had not been listening to my body for several months, why should it be a surprise if my body was now about to shout quite loudly, 'What did you expect?' We told both David and Daniel that they would be having another little friend joining them very soon, probably next weekend, but we did not know whether it was a boy or a girl. Both of them seemed to take it in their stride, an early indication of our experience in their teenage years when the word "whatever" seemed to come into its own. David had his music and his Playstation games to keep him interested, or a jigsaw if he was really stuck, so I don't recall him ever saying "I'm bored". Daniel had so much reading to preoccupy him that when I shared the news of the imminent arrival of a sibling, I could just as easily have uttered the words, "Leeds has just suffered a massive earthquake and no longer exists".

Barry rooted around in the loft space and in the garage, trying to locate various bags containing old baby clothes, as well as the travel cot, the little baby rocker, and some bedding. Much of the older clothing from when David was born had been passed on many years previously. White is always a good neutral colour. We just had to hope that the baby was not extremely long and very big, and with that in mind, we made a rush purchase of four white babygrows and a healthy supply of personal supplies for me and a packet of disposable nappies ready for the big day.

The Thursday came and sure enough my waters broke early

evening and I was admitted onto the maternity ward. Barry was with me and anxiously awaited the outcome. This time the labour was nowhere near as intensive, or at least that is how it seemed. Maybe we should have more, I thought, if it was going to be this easy. Maybe not. Shortly after midnight, amidst the groaning and pushing, I was on the cusp of delivering the baby. Both boys were no doubt fast asleep in bed, blissfully unaware of how new life comes into the world, and mum had probably fallen asleep in a spare bed in our house instead of sleeping in the annex. At twenty-five minutes past midnight, the plaintive little cries of a young baby girl announced her arrival. Lucy Ann Squit was born.

Almost immediately, we opted for the name Lucy, and with equal speed abbreviated it to Loos. With her lovely little fingers and delicate fingernails, she did not appear half as dirty as the boys when they were born. She was very quickly cleaned, weighed and handed back to me to put to my breast. Barry was beside himself, weeping with delight. He had a little girl. We had a little girl. She had a mop of dark moist hair, thankfully having the early finesse not to arrive with a mohican hairstyle.

Barry was able to get off home about an hour later leaving little Loos with me under the care of the staff on the maternity ward. The following day, Loos turned a little jaundiced so we had to stay in longer than we hoped, not coming home until the Sunday evening. David and Daniel thought their little sister was an adorable addition to the family and both were equally gentle and sensitive when they came to see me in hospital with mum on the Friday afternoon after school. I think they were more worried about the prospect of Barry cooking for them for a couple of days than anything else!

Loos was, and still is, a little darling. She was so delicate, weighing in at six pounds and a few ounces. She took to feeding very easily and rapidly put on weight, much to the satisfaction of the health visitor, who realised it would be one less child to worry about. Dressed in her little white babygrow, wrapped around with a crocheted blanket, she was the picture of innocence.

CHAPTER 34

AND SO...

...there you have it. The Squits' family history. With the arrival of Loos, there were the five of us, and with mum we were all settled in the lovely village of Ryme Intrinseca. Barry and I were proud to be the parents of three wonderful children. Daniel the child prodigy, David the creative musician, Loos brimming with potential. The cats, Semi and Franki, were remarkably quite agile even in 1999, bearing in mind that by then they must have been about twelve or thirteen.

We have been through lots of experiences together. I have shared with you about my upbringing, my childhood, and how Barry and I met. We have seen how Barry has made tremendous progress in his career, which has taken him to many foreign countries, my budding interest in the WI and in the Conservatives, and tentative involvement in the church. We have also shared some of the joyous experiences which many parents similarly experience: a child's first school play, the pride of seeing your child singing publicly for the first time, and the natural concern each of us has that our children will have broad interests which are not confined to academic achievement but will encompass enjoying sport and music and that they will able to interact and socialise with people of all age groups.

Which one of us knows how our child will turn out? We all hope that each of our children (or child if we have only one) will take their place in society and will contribute to the good of society and not be a conduit for evil. When Loos was born, Dave was just short of his tenth birthday and Daniel was nearly seven and a half (halves are very important when we are younger, aren't they?). The boys seemed well-adjusted but they were still only in the early stages of their journey into life. Who knew what the next years would bring?

AFTERWORD

Since Loos was born, seven years have passed. If "a week is a long time in politics" (if you follow Harold Wilson's observation), what is seven years in family life?

I hope to review the family's progress in another book and share with you all the exciting developments which happened during Dave's adolescence, Daniel's and Loos' amazing academic progress, and Barry's scary episode with the law.

We smile when we see various car stickers these days, don't we, and in that context, let me leave you with this thought: "A family is for life; not just for special occasions."

Printed in Great Britain
by Amazon